# CLOUDED JUDGEMENT

## TRENCH RAIDERS BOOK 5

## THOMAS WOOD

BOLEYNBENNETT PUBLISHING

Visit my website at www.ThomasWoodBooks.com

Printed in the United Kingdom

First Printing: April 2019
by
BoleynBennett Publishing

## GRAB ANOTHER BOOK FOR FREE

If you enjoy this book, why not pick up another one, completely free?

'Enemy Held Territory' follows Special Operations Executive Agent, Maurice Dumont as he inspects the defences at the bridges at Ranville and Benouville. Fast paced and exciting, this Second World War thriller is one you won't want to miss!
Details can be found at the back of this book.

# PART I

# 1

It had taken me no more than five minutes to sprint from the hospital to the village, my small and rather unprepared feet taking a battering each and every time I connected with the cobbled street below.

The village itself bore few of the scars of war that I had become so awfully accustomed to in recent months. It was true that there were a few damaged houses and upturned statues in the square, a result of a few wayward shells, but in the main, the village still seemed intact.

It was why I had continued to reside there, despite the fact that the war could creep up on this small French village any day now. It was a stubbornness that was shared by a great many of the locals, all of whom kept their heads firmly away from the windows, as my footsteps galloped down the darkened street.

"Come on. Come on. Nearly there."

I found myself interrupting my own thoughts, the

rancid breath that I breathed into the blackness of the night time disappearing as quickly as it had appeared.

I was close now, which was good news, as I wasn't entirely sure for how much longer I could keep on running.

I tripped up as I looked around to see how much further I had to go. I could see the front door that I was aiming for, I could only hope that a small lamp would be lit on the table as I approached.

I found my footing and continued on in earnest, not slowing down a bit as I got to the door. My feet slipped as I came to a halt, the soles of my shoes burning my skin as if I had been walking on hot coals.

I hammered on the door with the side of my fist, so hard that I imagined the old, rotting door might suddenly give way, and my arm would pulverise its way through it.

There was no lamp on the table. Not from what I could see. Not yet anyway.

I thumped again and again, until I heard the noise that I had been dreaming of for the last hour or so. The lock behind the aging, frail door, began to unlock itself in a state of sleepy confusion, or that was all I could account for, as it seemed to take an age to simply slide the bolts backwards.

The figure that revealed itself from behind the sodden wood appeared as just as confused as the unlocking door, despite the fact that I could not see a single one of his facial features. I just knew that his body mass was somewhere behind it.

I gave the figure no opportunity to ask me in, or reject my entry, as I tumbled through the doorframe, forcing the figure to stumble backwards with me.

I slammed the door back into its frame, with a gentleness, carefully and considerately sliding the bolts back across, jut in case another figure had been some way off behind me.

His eyes began to glow in the dark, as if they were only just getting going, before he squinted, troubled.

"Emilie?" he whispered, his warm breath splashing my reddened face. "Emilie Barrot?"

"Oui, Monsieur Roussir," I gasped, "It is me."

He fumbled around in the darkness for a moment, before the candle was lit and held up to my face. The flame flickered and burned so vehemently that I had to look away for a moment, the heat doing nothing to help me recover from the sprint that I had just completed.

"My girl, what are you doing here, at this time of the night?"

"I am sorry. I had nowhere else to go. I do not have long to explain."

Michel Roussir's eyebrows furrowed together at the news, great lines of concern etching from one side of his forehead to the other. I could tell immediately that he was already worrying about what he would do once I had departed. I was certain that the candle would burn for many hours after I had left him.

He nodded his head towards the centre of the room, "You better sit down, my girl."

The heat of the candle left my face momentarily, at which point I discovered that I was beginning to shiver. My body had cooled down dramatically in the thirty seconds or so since I had stopped running, to the point where I was now experiencing the other extreme, my cheeks now losing the reddened pigment that had burned a moment before.

As I made my way over to the table, Monsieur Roussir noticed the small box that I held firmly in my grasp, as he began eyeing it with a suspicion that told me he was more than intrigued, he was fascinated.

It was a small box, with a simple hinge lid that I had used for years to store little trinkets and necklaces within, but in recent months had received a renewed sense of purpose.

It was buried in a nearby forest, far enough in so that no one would stumble upon it, but near enough to the outskirts so that I could grab it at a moment's notice. Which is what I had done immediately before running to Monsieur Roussir's home.

"I could not get to anyone else in time. They are probably watching my family anyway."

"Who are, my girl?"

He knew exactly who I meant, yet I found myself spelling it out for him anyway, in a hushed whisper, in case any of them were stacked up outside the door.

"The Germans."

At their mention, his eyes fell back on the small trinket box that sat before him, its former glory dulled quite considerably by the deposits of dirt that still clung to its sides. Even still, it was easy to see, even in the meagre light of a single candle, of how it glistened and sparkled in days gone by.

I could tell that he had already sussed what was inside the box. It wouldn't have taken a genius to work it out.

"Money?" he queried, nodding towards the box, as if I needed a reminder as to what was the subject of his consciousness.

I nodded.

"Quite a lot of it too."

His eyes sparkled, more than the box had ever done before.

I had earned more money in the last few months of this war, than I had done in the preceding twenty-four years of my life, each franc having sat patiently in the box until a time when I felt safe enough to use it.

It was sufficient to say that I was not yet safe enough to use it. But someone else might be able to.

The money, of which I had lost count long ago, was more than I could ever have earned from nursing. The job that I had fallen into as a result of this war was hard work and harrowing, but I was certainly not repaid in financial terms.

This side job was my secret.

Everyone that I knew had one, but sometimes it was best to just keep them hidden. Every now and then, one would find its way to the surface, plucked by the fishing line of an inquisitive neighbour or nosey best friend. Some secrets did more harm than good, while others still, ruined lives.

Which was exactly why I had tied a millstone to my secret and had allowed it to sink to the bottom of the ocean as much as I could.

"Monsieur Roussir," I breathed, my chest still heaving and having a great deal of trouble in recouping all of my lost oxygen. "This box here," I rested my hand on it for effect, "there is a large sum of money in it. I entrust it to you now."

I raised an eyebrow, in the hope that I would get some sort of a reaction from the man. I had no such luck.

"The money inside is for my family. I would like you to give it to them, with the message that I want them to use it to get away from here. To get away from the war. There is enough money here for them to start anew."

He continued to stare at me blankly, and I almost asked him to repeat back to me what I had said. But then, he blinked. He was still alive at least.

"Please, Monsieur Roussir. It must be given to them. You can take for yourself what you like. There is plenty to go around."

Suddenly, he sprung into life, as much as he could do at this hour of the night, as he placed his hand firmly on top of mine, which was still clinging tightly to the box.

"I will see it done, my girl."

"Thank you, Monsieur Roussir."

"May I ask how you came about such money, my girl. Forgive me, but you are only a nurse and I did not think that you were paid quite so handsomely."

He must have seen the suspicion that was tinting my vision for a moment, as he added "What am I to tell your family, if they were to ask?"

I knew that I could trust the kindly old gentleman who sat across from me, his face a contortion of old wrinkles, made deeper by the shadows that danced across his face in the candlelight.

I would need to make it brief, I was certain that I did not have too much longer.

"Last year, when the hospital was first moved here, there was a woman who lived nearby. She approached me one day to ask me if I would do some work for her, aside from my nursing duties. At first, I merely thought that she was inquisitive. Interested in what happened up at the hospital. I thought maybe she was looking for a relative."

"But she was not?"

"No, quite the opposite. She was waiting for a German, a Major, who was due to stop by at some point. She wanted to know when preparations were made for his arrival."

"And...what happened?"

"Well, I told her. She was paying me a lot of money after all. But nothing much happened after that. I merely assumed it was all harmless. But after a few more requests, it did not take long to work out what was happening."

He was not a naïve man, but he was hungry for every detail, something that I was careful not to give him.

"She continued to pay me for the rest of the year, in exchange for brief reports on the number of soldiers that I saw pass through and any whispers that came from dying German's mouths. Anything really that might be helpful to her contacts."

"Who were her contacts?"

"She never said. But I always assumed the British."

He looked puzzled for a moment, as if he was confused as to why she would be talking to someone across the channel. For a brief second, I thought that he maybe had no knowledge whatsoever that there was a war on, his questions were angled in such a way.

"She went quiet over Christmas. I did not hear a thing from her. Then, she reappeared about a month ago. She wanted to know some very specific things. Things that meant I would have to go looking for the answers. It was risky..."

"And now you must leave, my girl."

"*Oui,* Monsieur Roussir. I must leave. You will make sure that my family receive the money?"

He looked at me, with a reassuring smile etched across his face, "Every franc, my girl."

He placed both hands on top of mine and as I stared into his deep, hazel coloured eyes, I knew that he meant every word. He would not take a single franc for himself.

I felt quite bad for the old man, not just because I

was leaving a huge weight upon his shoulders, but because of what I had kept hidden from him. I had told him what he had needed to know, what my family needed to know, but I hadn't told him the whole truth.

I had failed to mention all the preparations at the hospital for what was to come, the extra training and teaching that we had received and the huge canisters that had been passing along the supply routes nearby. I had neglected to mention what it was exactly that had been asked of me and why it now meant that I must leave.

But all of that would have to wait. At least until the end of the war and maybe even longer.

For now, I had to leave. I had to run again. But the next person I was hoping to get to was going to be a little bit riskier.

"*Au revoir,* Monsieur Roussir."

"Goodbye, Emilie. Good luck, my girl."

I slipped away from his house and began to run in the direction that I had just come, before I heard the unmistakeable sound of German troops heading my way.

## 2

It took me a further twenty minutes or so to make it to the hospital, after I avoided several groups of German troops who were scouring the nearby area for anyone that was out when they shouldn't have been.

The Germans seemed to have no real reason to impose so strict a curfew upon us as they did, every one of them not giving a sufficient reply when asked. However, it seemed as if they did not need a reason for many of the new laws that they had impressed upon us, from the order to simply keep our streets clean and tidy, to the way that German officers were owed a salute every time they walked past.

For some reason, the military discipline that was instilled in every German troop that I saw, was being extended upon the occupied civilians, much to their disgust.

It was all part of the reason why I had begun to accept some of the money in return for information. I frequently wondered where in the world my information went to and whether it was ever put to any use. Maybe the woman that I had met had been a fraud and had not worked for anyone at all. But then, how would she have had access to such large sums of money?

She was certainly working for someone, somewhere, but I was yet to see a direct result of any of my information that was being passed on. There was a real possibility however, that after what had happened in the last few hours, that I was bound to at least hear of some sort of results.

I knew the route from the village to the hospital so well that I could have run it blindfolded, which was just as well, owing to the inky darkness that had been spilled across the length of the skyline that night.

The hospital itself was set in the grounds of a grand chateau, that had once housed the mayor of the local commune. Sturdy tents had been erected, in and around the gardens, for those soldiers who merely required an element of recuperation, before being sent back to the frontline.

It was inside the chateau itself that the wards and surgical rooms were located, with hundreds of men passing through its doors every week, with varying types of injuries and diseases.

It was within these walls that I had started to build something of a life for myself, having been trained as a nurse and worked there for the last seven months. I had seen everything, from men gasping and screaming as they died, to men taking nothing more than a slight glance at the stump of an arm that they would now have for the rest of their lives.

The look at a stump was an odd one, that I had observed many times now. It was a look of almost total dejection, at the realisation that their lives would never be the same again, they would not be able to do the things that they had been able to do just hours before.

But often, it was also an expression of over-whelming jubilation, of victory almost. It meant that they had beaten death. They were staring down at death's best attempt at plucking them from this realm and yet, somehow, they had come out on top. Their war was over. They would be one of the survivors.

From then on, they would be filled with glee and excitement, looking forward to the day that they would be discharged and sent back to their homes, to their families.

It was those men that I would have to try earnestly to avoid. Even at such a late hour, there was bound to be one or two of them awake, who would call out in the darkness at the invisible beauty that they thought was lurking somewhere in the corners of the ward.

If that happened, then there was a chance that the people that would soon be after me, would catch me before I could even start running.

I knew that the one person that I did want to see would be within these great corridors somewhere along the way. She would more than likely be sitting in her small room, by the light of an overly-loud and exhausting gas lamp, writing up various reports and preparing for the day ahead. I knew exactly what she would be doing as I had been there hundreds of times myself before.

As I approached her room, I could already hear the sound of a striking match through the half-opened door. It was done by all of us so that we could hear the calls of a frightened man in the middle of the night.

I waited for a moment, allowing enough time for the cigarette to be lit and a few drags to be taken, before I pushed the door further ajar.

"Marie."

It was a low whisper, so low that it could have been mistaken for a voice inside one's head, but the jump with which she rose from her chair suggested it was more akin to a gunshot.

"Emilie!" she exclaimed, after almost burning her top lip on the glowing stick that stood to attention from her mouth. It seemed almost as frightened as Marie did. Her hands shook as she had dropped the pen that she had been using to the floor, leaving a nice big splash of blue ink on the ground for her to clean up. "What are you doing here?"

She tried to calm herself down as best she could, which is always easier said than done, especially when your body begins to realise that there is no threat whatsoever, and your flustered heart continues to pound.

I felt bad that I had made her sweat in that way, but I had no other alternatives. There was no other way of going about it.

Marie was one of my best friends at the hospital. She was a better nurse than I was and had been honing her skills for several years before I had completed my training, but she was always there for me, a far more approachable figure than some of the newer nurses who felt like they were superior to me.

"It is a long story," I tried to explain, but I could not bring myself to go through the whole story once again that night. Marie would simply have to make do with vague outlines and assumptions. I was surprised that she had not seen something like this coming along one day, and I supposed that I was far better at standing on top of that secret than I had previously thought.

"I just need you to take these two letters. Promise me that you will send them immediately. They are very important."

"Why can't you just send them?" she spat back, her cigarette almost falling from her mouth. She was a kind soul, but her abruptness had landed her in trouble on more than one occasion. It was part of the reason why I had taken to her.

"I need to go away. I am going now. I won't have time to send them. Here, I will pay."

I shoved the money into her palm, along with the two letters, before almost sprinting away to leave her with no choice but to take them.

I would just have to trust her that she wouldn't open and read the letters.

"Goodbye, Marie. I am sorry to have made you jump."

"But—"

It was already too late, by the time the first syllable had come from her mouth, I was gone. Back into the darkness.

As my feet slid over the highly varnished floors of the entrance hall of the chateau, I recalled the first time that I had met the woman, the one that had changed my life forever.

It was not long after I had joined the hospital, and I was rushing about trying to find some more bedsheets for the new intake of wounded men, that were due to come in once the latest offensive had faltered.

She stood some way off, but she locked eyes with me immediately, beckoning me over with them, the second that we connected.

As I approached her, I realised that she had a kindly face, but one with eyes so stern that one could only do exactly as she said. She seemed like a school-teacher of some sort.

"*Goeiedag.*"

I assumed that the woman who now stood before me was Flemish, as we had a lot of people wandering through this part of France as they searched for a new home, but she did not seem to give off that sort of impression.

I replied in the best Flemish that I could muster, only being able to speak certain phrases, more to help me get by in my professional capacity than any other conversation.

We spoke for a while after that, which had led to

me slowly becoming one of her feeders of information. Gradually, we became close, before I learned that she was, in fact, a Dutch woman who was merely here to make the best of the opportunity that was presented before her.

She could speak several languages, as could I, and we took great enjoyment of having conversations in three or more languages before we tired of one another, and retired for the evening. It was this fact that had made it difficult for me to select which language I should write to her in.

*It is time for me to go, I am afraid. I would like you to know that it is not through want that I leave you, but through necessity. It was just one step too far for me. If you see the necessity also, then I will not hold you back in making the same decision that I did.*

*I hope with all my heart that once this is all over, we can meet up again and discuss things more fully.*

I had no name for her, no idea of her background, other than the address that we shared our brief meetings in, as we relayed information to one another. It was all that I could scribble on the envelope in such a hurry.

I had been as vague as I possibly could have been, without it being void of any indication of where I had really gone. She must have known that the risks involved in me merely sending a letter at all would be enough to give her the general notion of its contents.

I really did want to meet up with her after the war

was ended, however. Even if it was just to find out her name.

Deliberately, I tried to tell myself that I had written just the one letter, as I could not bring myself to recall the other one that I had handed to Marie. If I was to mull it over in my mind for too long, it would sadden me too much, possibly even bring tears to my eyes, at which point I would be putting my life in an unnecessary danger.

It was all too complicated to be thinking about right now anyway. I was a French nurse, that was feeding information to a Dutch woman, who in turn was taking the information to whoever she pleased. He was a German soldier. There was nothing more to him than that.

But it was all a little too complex to be giving it too much attention right now.

Instead, I had to focus on simply putting one foot in front of the other one and making sure that I carried myself as far away from that hospital as I possibly could.

Instead of engaging my thoughts with the letters that I had written, I pulled out his *flachmann,* the hip flask that he had entrusted me with when he had last been back behind the frontline.

I twisted it and rubbed it over in my palm with such a vigour that I thought I would need to get it repaired soon enough, I was that convinced that it was beginning to wear thin. I looked at the dulled steel as it slowly warmed in my hands, just catching the desperate glow of the moonlight as it peered through the clouds.

It was empty and I didn't think that it had housed a single droplet of the stuff in quite a while, but it somehow made me feel warmer inside. It was as if the small *flachmann* that Franck had given to me was somehow keeping me safe, keeping me sane even.

There was no way that it had had any real influence over my life, and yet I found myself believing in its abilities to somehow keep a watch over me. I wondered if Franck had ever taken a similar comfort from it, when it had been in his hands.

It was his face that I tried to recall as I gripped hold of it tightly, his round, almost gaunt face glaring back at me from the wall of the flask.

I needed to cover a great distance tonight if I was to have any chance of survival, if I was to ever have a chance of seeing Franck's face again, in the flesh.

What I wanted, what I really wanted, was to be able to get to England. The promised land. But even I, the young nurse who was seeing her loved one's face in the side of a hip flask, knew full well that that was impossible.

There was nothing for it but to simply trek eastwards, towards the rising sun.

# PART II

# 1

I was back in the trench and it felt good. It felt really good.

Over the past couple of weeks, I had found my life particularly difficult to deal with, with hundreds, if not thousands of questions racing through my mind every single minute. But the instant that I had my feet back in a German trench, every single one of those questions, every tiny little doubt that I had ever harboured, was completely dispelled, eradicated to a non-existence.

The raid itself had felt no different to any of the others that I had previously been on, everything seemed to be going as smoothly as it possibly could do. The wire had been cut almost perfectly, to the point where it looked like a seamstress had done it and we had managed to slide into the trench with an almost perfect silence. Even the new boys were performing well.

We dispatched of a few sentries who were more milling about in the frontline, trying to keep warm, than they were keeping watch, all the while still maintaining a decent level of noiselessness that I had previously thought completely impossible.

Everything was going so well, that I thought I even caught Captain Arnold smiling somewhere in the darkness, his eyes glistening as if he had just received the best news of his life. I took a greater appreciation of him for a moment, as I looked at the tall, enthusiastic and driven man that was leading me into battle.

At first, he had seemed off with me, distant to a degree, but over the last couple of days I had realised what a terrific officer he truly was, the possessor of a fearlessness that seemed to only come with men of his calibre.

It was this sense of security, the notion of how easy everything seemed to be, that would get me into the most trouble, however. As I carelessly began flicking through documents and folders that the Captain had unearthed for me to sift through, I noticed that I was gradually losing interest in the actual content of the papers and more intrigued by the visions that were filling my mind.

The great landscapes and forests that I had grown up around, were slowly coming into focus in my mind, including the vibrant colours of springtime, mixed with the harshest of winters that I had ever experienced. The smell of the damp, cold December nights, infused with the summer rainfall, stirred up all kinds of emotions within the pits of my stomach.

It was only once the grand landscapes had been painted in my mind, that I began to populate them, to slot figures in who had been a part of my life and who I was missing terribly.

My mother and father, as poor as they were, were both immeasurably happy and, despite the fact that I had not seen them for many months, their smiles were just as prominent and recognisable as if I had seen them just yesterday.

I began to long to be back with them again, in the outstretched arms of my mother and within earshot of my father's terribly coarse jokes that were not meant for my ears. It was a life before the war, one that was not tainted by thoughts of artillery shells or machinegun bullets, severed limbs or ugly deaths.

It was a life that I never thought that I would get to see again and now, here it was, appearing before my very eyes while I ransacked a German trench.

Within a flash, the whole beautiful and dreamlike landscape was washed away, to the point where it felt like it had never been there.

The warm, welcoming feeling, that had slowly taken a grip over my insides, was immediately banished, replaced by a chill that could only come with the sight that I was met with.

There was a dark shadow coming towards me, like the hooded outline of Death as he slowly made his way towards me. Foolishly, I looked for his scythe, as if somehow comforted by the fact that he had forgotten the most rudimental instrument in the whole of his arsenal.

The figure slowly came into focus, the German uniform now totally unmistakeable amid the darkened khaki of my own. He bore down on me, his face rolled up into a snarl, like I was vermin that had somehow snuck into his kitchen.

And, like vermin, he intended to exterminate me, in the swiftest way possible.

There was nothing that I could do now apart from wait. Expectantly, I stood there awaiting my fate, which I supposed would be a relatively quick and almost pain free death.

I tried to send some sort of a signal down to my toes, to begin waggling and get my feet into gear, but either my feet simply refused, or the message never got to its intended recipient, because I continued to stand and stare at the oncoming man.

I was fully aware that I was frozen, the phenomena of which had never happened to me before, but there seemed to be nothing that I could do to swing myself into action.

It would have been so easy for me to lift up my wooden cosh and bring it down on his head, or to bring my revolver to bear and fire a few rounds into his gut.

But none of that happened. I was completely rooted to the spot.

The man, for obvious reasons, saw no real threat in

my existence and so chose not to execute me straight away. It was a fair analysis of the situation, I was far more likely to do away with the ones who were more likely to shoot me, than the coward who would not.

Instead of the flash of a revolver as it exploded in my face, my vision was filled with a fist the size of a football, and I felt my nose crumple as it gave way to the force with which the man had connected with me.

There was only a brief moment where the pain that ballooned across my face was registered, before I felt myself take a couple of steps backwards and hit the wall of the trench.

After that, there was nothing. There was no noise, no pain, no sights or smells of home. Just a perfect silence. It was almost heavenly to me.

I do not know for how long it was that I lay there unconscious, but once I had regained my senses, I simply lay there for a second or two, trying to work out what had happened.

I had a perfect recall of the events leading up to my knockout, but I listened carefully for any signs of a German victory, in which case I would have to be excruciatingly careful in the way that I went about things.

My unconscious state must have lasted for less than three or four seconds, for I soon found myself staring at the back of the German's head, as he beat my sergeant within an inch of his life at the bottom of the trench.

With a renewed sense of courage and bravery, I

pulled my revolver up and lined it up perfectly with the back of the German's skull, all I had to do now was pull the trigger.

But there was something stopping me. A respect for the German for sneaking up on us? A sudden unwillingness to take another human life? I do not know. The only thing that I am sure of however, was that it manifested itself as a quiver in my hand, one so fierce and unceasing, that even when I gripped my wrist with my free hand, it continued to wobble the revolver around, to the point where I was useless.

Eventually, I felt my arms slump forward as the weight of the revolver dragged them back towards the ground. I was defeated. Completely and utterly.

I wanted no more part in this war. I wanted no more of the killing and destruction that I had been called to inflict on my fellow man in recent months. I was done.

I did not even care for the life of the sergeant who lay struggling beneath the weight of the German, who was slowly pressing down on his throat with such a ferocity that he would have been seeing stars almost straight away.

I cared not for his wife or children, nor for the rest of the men in the trench that I was putting at risk. As long as I was not the one pulling the trigger, then I did not care what happened to the rest of them.

My perception of time was completely thrown out of the window, as it felt like hours before anyone did anything to remedy my mistakes, when in reality it can't have been much more than two or three seconds.

It was so difficult for me to feel anything at all other than a complete desperation, that I completely ignored the imposing stature of Captain Arnold as he made his way over to me. I had no real interest in the fact that he was raising his wooden cosh up high as he raced towards me. I took no notes over the way in which he brought the baton down hard on the German's head, bringing him to a crumpling mess of flesh at my feet.

And I certainly took no pride whatsoever when I pushed the steel of a bayonet straight through the wincing German's chest. I had started to feel nothing towards anyone but myself.

If it wasn't for me, if only I had managed to keep my head and stayed focused on the task at hand, then two of our boys would have made it through that night. The chances are that in all likelihood, they would have been killed on the very next outing, as they were both rookies, but I should have been the one that had given them that chance.

Peterson was the first one to buy it that night, taking an incredibly lucky round in his body somewhere as the German tumbled to the ground. I was so focused on the body lying at my feet that I didn't even realise that the gun had erupted, until it was far too late for young Peterson.

It is a shame. He seemed like such a nice young lad. But it was me who killed him.

The other was Dornan. Reg, I think his first name was. He was struck by a machinegun round that pierced through the top of his thigh. Or maybe it was a bit of shrapnel. I'm not sure. Whatever it was, it killed him, nonetheless. I killed him.

If only I had the courage to carry on with my job, to push the things of old to the back of my mind, just for a few hours, then there was a chance that those boys would still be here today. But I didn't, and that was what made me begin to think in the way that I did.

I saw no point in carrying on with this awful war any longer, where the life expectancy was more down to luck than skill or ability.

If I had done my job, then my conscience would be clear. But it isn't.

It is why I am fully understanding of where I am right now, Andrew, and why I wholeheartedly deserve to be in this situation. I appreciate yours, and the Captain's, efforts in trying to buoy me and keep me positive.

But, at the same time, I keep asking myself the same question, over and over again.

How can I possibly expect to be free from it all, if I don't accept the punishment? And, if that punishment is to be death, then so be it. It is my fault and mine alone. You should feel no guilt in the matter whatsoever.

I hope to see you soon Andrew and that you are recovering in Old Blighty as well as you can.

*McKay.*

## 2

I began to fold up the letter that I had received from McKay and proceeded to slot it into my top pocket, for safe keeping.

I had read and re-read it numerous times now, at least once a day if I could help it, as each time that I read it through, a great weight felt like it had been lifted from my shoulders.

There was something within that letter, some sort of sentiment, that made me feel like I had not been responsible for all the death and destruction that I had caused in this war. Somehow, it helped me to externalise some of the blame, in the same way that McKay had started to take some of it upon himself.

I tried not to dwell on the actual events of the letter too much, nor did I linger on what came after the events detailed in McKay's scribblings. We all knew what happened; McKay stole some maps and put them in the German frontline trench. It was not a big deal, not to us anyway.

We trusted him and, knowing exactly what had gone through his mind as he battled with himself, had made me trust him even more. It was refreshing to know that he had identified his mistakes, but not only that, he was now accepting of the potential punishment that he might face.

I wondered if he had conjured up enough courage to send a similar letter to Captain Arnold, detailing everything that had happened and admitting his faults. But, then again, it wouldn't have surprised me if I was to discover that Captain Arnold had completely forgotten the episode altogether by now. He almost certainly would have forgotten Privates Dornan and Peterson.

I had remembered their names being mentioned briefly when I had first joined the team, but I felt like I had got to know them far better since they had been killed, than I would ever have been able to when they were alive.

McKay had sent me many other letters, detailing some of his conversations with the men who have since been and gone, and on more than one occasion I felt quite emotional and affected by the way in which he spoke of them. I wondered if he would have similarly kind words to say about me if I was to die before he did.

It had been relatively easy for me to stay in touch with McKay, from the confines of a hospital bed, and I was glad that we had done so. More than anything, it was a chance for me to take my mind away from the monotony of hospital life, the regimented lifestyle of meals and exercise times that were far more infuriating than the rigmaroles of military life.

My wounds had been serious enough to send me back to Britain, where the two puncture wounds in my thigh were treated properly, as far away from the front-line as possible and the hole in my hand stitched up nicely.

Over the weeks that I was restricted to lying in that hospital bed, it had given me plenty of time to think and write to McKay. We had grown closer in the month or so that we had spent apart than we had done in the months living in close contact with one another. It got to the point where we were missing each other's company.

The physical wounds that I had healed up better than I expected them to, but more than that, my mind was feeling refreshed, I was feeling ready to go back.

The echoes and voices of Bob Sargent, that I had heard reverberate around my mind, were gone, so too were the incapacitating headaches and the unquench-able desires to take a sip from my hip flask.

It was that last one that I was relishing in more than anything else. It felt like I was a free man, as if the chains had been released and I was able to break free from the pain and trauma that the paraffin was causing me.

I was excited to go back, to be able to see how

much of a better soldier I could be without the influence of the alcohol surging around my body.

*If only Bob could see me now.*

I had managed to shake off the necessity of the paraffin, after many sleepless nights and many more headache-filled mornings, but the feeling of something missing burned a hole in my top pocket, more than it had done before.

The absence of the hip flask was still troubling me, as I still felt like I had not really achieved anything without it.

The hip flask itself had seen me through many different episodes, where most other men had ended up dead and then, the one time that I did not have it on my person, I ended up almost bleeding to death in a hospital somewhere in France.

I still had not heard from the others about how they had managed to get me away. All of their letters detailing the matters had been subjected to the most stringent of censors.

In fact, I did not know if we had lost anyone on our last journey, as I had simply not heard from any of them. The last I had seen of Earnshaw was blood gushing from his leg like a stream, as we left him propped up behind some debris in No Man's Land. That had been the last that I had seen or heard of him.

The only reason why had I managed to receive and send messages to McKay was because I knew where he was.

Shortly after being released from the hospital,

recovering from his own wounds sustained as a result of my neglect, McKay was arrested by the military police. For the last two weeks, he had been in a cell somewhere near Albert, which was where I could only assume that everyone else was.

I reasoned that the motivations for locking McKay up were as a result of the deal that Captain Arnold had rather foolishly agreed to, before our last outing together.

He had promised his superior officers that McKay would be dead before the sun came up, which was, fortunately for McKay, not the case. Therefore, I supposed that the normal protocol must now apply, and that McKay was being held in a cell as he waited for the date of his court martial to be agreed upon.

I was hoping that it was proving difficult to set a date, when the rest of the team were being routinely sent out on operation after operation. Maybe that would mean that McKay would stay locked up forever.

It was along this train of thought that I wondered what would happen if all the witnesses of that night were killed, before it was brought before the courts. It wasn't entirely impossible. Maybe that was his only way out alive.

I did the button up on my top pocket where I had just placed McKay's letter, a worthy replacement, I thought, for the hip flask that had caused me, and so many others, so many issues.

I gave it a couple of taps for no real reason, as I started to step down onto the gangplank. I had enjoyed my time back in Britain, it had helped straighten myself out in more than one regard, but I was an absent sergeant, to a group of men who needed me desperately, so I was looking forward to getting back to them.

The hustle and bustle in the port was absolutely tremendous, and I could not help but smile to myself as I was met by a sea of khaki uniforms and burly shouts.

*It feels good to be back.*

I rebuked myself almost instantly for feeling that way but, in truth, I had started to forget the horrors of war and replaced them in my mind with happy memories, of the laughs that I had shared with the rest of the team and how I had considered each one of them like a brother to me.

It was not the war that I had missed, but the men in that war that my heart was pining for.

Even though I was still many miles away from a reunion with those men, it at least felt good to be surrounded by men dressed in a similar fashion, each one of them knowing what might be expected of them in the coming weeks and months.

The boys who stepped off the ship with me were, in the main, wounded soldiers who had recovered and were now eager to get back to the frontline. There was, however, a large proportion of newly-trained, untested soldiers, some of whom barely looked a day over the age of twelve.

Each of them stepped off the ship smiling and

joking with their friends, masking the true fear and desperation that lurked beneath the surface. None of them wanted to be here, every single one of them would say that this was what they had wanted, but all of them had joined up because he knew of someone else signing up, and he wouldn't go without them.

The smiles and cheery faces that were masking their true terror was swiftly snatched from them, as Sergeants and Corporals all around, erupted like an artillery bombardment, yanking them into line and order.

I couldn't help but pity the boys that were subjected to their wrath.

Life here was going to be very different to the one that they had experienced back in Britain.

Life in Britain had seemed to have carried on as normal, as normal as you can when millions of men are fighting just a few hundred miles away.

It was a nation that was, however, closer to us boys in France than we had first thought. Back in the closing stages of the year before, the German navy had bombed some coastal towns in the north and everyone was pulling their weight behind the war effort, men and women, young and old.

In recent months the Germans even had the audacity to fly over in their Zeppelins to drop bombs on innocent civilians, which only served in uniting everyone together, as a whole, to get behind the lads in khaki.

Although at war, there was a real sense of unity and

harmony between everyone that I spoke to back in Britain.

The rosy-like hue that tinted my short break back in Britain was furthered by the brief time that I had to spend with my family.

Not one of them had been notified in any way that I was injured, never mind the fact that I was in Britain, and I cursed the postal service for losing so many of my correspondences. I knew that I could not kid them however, all of them knew that I was lying through my teeth. It was good to see them, nonetheless.

My mother, father and sister were all still their usual selves, trying to plod along in their lives and make the most of what they had been given. The street that I had grown up on in Southampton was more or less exactly how I had left it, but without the boys kicking things down the street or chasing each other up it.

As it turned out, three families had already been notified that their boys would not be coming home. Mother had become the official family lookout for the telegraph boy, who would bring news of my own demise.

"Name?"

"Andrew Ellis. Sergeant. 4945821."

I replied curtly but politely to the corporal in charge of a long list of names.

*Nice work if you can get it.*

"Date of birth?"

"Twelfth June 1896."

The corporal managed to locate my name, alongside the thousands of others that must have been there, before guiding me through the various queues and corridors to get me to where I needed to be.

But there was one thing that was bugging me the whole time that he was talking.

I had somehow missed my nineteenth birthday.

*Happy Birthday to you.*

## 3

My journey back toward Albert was an uneventful one, full of endless military checks broken up by a series of dozing. For some reason, since I had been in the hospital, I had found it almost impossible to go through a full day without getting my head down for a short period. It was one of the things that I had trained my body to become accustomed to, a custom that I did not think would be able to continue once I met up with everyone once again.

I had spent much of the time thinking of my family yet again and what I might put in a letter to my sister, once I got around to it. For some reason, the draw of writing to her, rather than my parents, was more appealing, as if it was some sort of penance over the fact that I had almost forgotten her for so long.

She was a kind-hearted soul, my sister, but one that did not seem to want for much in her life. She was more than happy to simply plod along and marry the first man who paid her any attention. It was not that she had not received any attention that was the cause for her current marital status, but the fact that she was only just approaching seventeen and still some way off being considered an eligible woman.

Over the years we had shared in one another's annoyances with our parents, spending hours upon hours wandering around the docks, taking in the sights and bemoaning the latest episode of the horrors of childhood.

I had been prepared for many more years of walks such as those, however, the sense of duty, the pull of the fight had become too strong for me and I had signed up within a few hours of me making my decision.

It was the first time in a long time that I had given some consideration to my life before the army, albeit the few days before I joined up.

There was a growing tension in the air, the talk of war filling every public house and butcher's shop throughout the whole town.

"It will be a war like no other," some had muttered, which had been met with a general agreement.

"You won't see my young Walter anywhere near one of them recruiting shops, you mark my words," muttered one woman as I worked, blissfully unaware of the fact that Walter had already accepted the King's shilling. He was one of the three who had already been killed on my street.

I did not feel like I had had my youth snatched

from me, rather it was an acceleration towards my adulthood, my rite of passage a few months before anyone else. Even so, I still missed those walks with my sister.

I walked alone now, through the rubble and debris that was the town of Albert. I had been dropped off half a mile or so behind the lines, and so had a walk of around two or so miles further back, before I got to Albert. The army's sense of direction had always confused me somewhat.

As I approached the village, I could make out the tall, imposing and impressive outline of the basilica, as it glistened gently in front of the sun that set my eyes streaming.

The walls that had once housed the ardent and enthusiastic prayers of the faithful still lay in ruins around the base of the church, the hallways and stairways down towards the crypt now out in the open air.

A couple of children scurried up and down the ramps that had been created in the rubble, each child daring to reach higher up than the last. I supposed they would be at it until sundown, as they still had quite a number of feet to go before they got to the top.

It was the figure that defiantly stood stretching out over the top of the basilica that, as always, stole my gaze. The figurine of the Madonna, clutching tightly to her child, continued to lean over to one side, as if it was defying the principle of gravity itself.

But, as I moved closer to it, I realised that it had been reinforced since I had last seen it, a mixture of poles and ropes ensuring that it wasn't to topple on one of the children's heads.

*That's a shame. I wanted it to come down, sharpish.*

It hadn't just been the lone Tommy who had told me the superstition about how the war would continue until it fell, but it seemed everyone in the nearby vicinity seemed convinced of it as fact. There had apparently even been some protests when the workmen had secured the statue to the top, with many bemoaning the fact that the war was now doomed to continue forever.

I chuckled softly, as I took a great comfort that I was not the only man on the Western Front who had taken an unhealthy interest in superstition and talismans.

*Maybe it wasn't the paraffin after all.*

I stood and took in the scene of the ruined basilica for a few more minutes, before I decided that I would soon have to tear myself away from it and find my destination.

"Oi! What you lookin' at?"

For a moment, the noise did not sound human, but within a flash, I slowly deciphered the tones to realise that it was a voice, a man's voice and, he was speaking English.

I turned, only to be met by the largest grin that I think I had ever seen in my life before. His face was clean and plump, as if he had been gorging himself on the finest foods in recent weeks, which I knew can't have been the case.

"Harry!" I exclaimed excitedly, genuinely delighted to see the man that stood before me. "I thought you were going to be dead!"

"So did I," chirped back Earnshaw, "Doctor's soon saw me right though."

"Last time I saw you, you looked like you were going to be at the pearly gates by the afternoon. Hit in the leg, weren't you?"

"Yeah," he replied, quite sheepishly, "turns out it wasn't quite as serious as it looked. Don't tell the others though, will you?"

"You mean, they haven't figured it out?"

"Not yet."

I chuckled and slapped him on the shoulder.

"Here to walk me home then? If you can manage it, of course."

"Oh, I'm really glad you're back."

We laughed and joked for the five-minute walk back towards our billet, in which time Earnshaw filled me in on all the comings and goings of recent weeks, so that I wasn't met with a huge surprise the minute that I walked through the door.

Somehow, no one had been killed since I had been gone. But, then again, it seemed like the whole team would be in the doghouse until the court martial, as they hadn't really done anything apart from standard patrols for the last fortnight.

"We're hoping something will change soon," surmised Earnshaw, as we slid through the door.

"I'm sure it will," I replied as I realised how much I

had missed the non-descript walls and frankly horrific odour of sweating men, that seemed to leak out of every crevice in the entire building.

"Look who I found, wandering the streets like a lost little cat," announced Earnshaw as I stepped into the room.

A mish mash of voices suddenly sparked up, to accompany the turning heads, as sounds of jubilation and cheeriness were interspersed with "Ellis!" and "Andrew!"

I immediately began to feel even better than I had done before, to the point where I became convinced that I could have recovered quicker in two weeks had I done it here in this room, as opposed to some over-packed ward back in Britain.

I shook hands and slapped backs for what felt like a good hour, as each one of them took it in turns to reintroduce their happy little faces to me once again.

"You two decided to stick around then?" I asked as Sergeant Lawrence appeared before me, his Canadian compatriot, Chester, not too far behind him.

"We figured you chumps would need us a lot more than anyone else on this side of the wire."

"Well, by my calculations," I retorted as I gripped Chester's hand, "more of us ended up in hospitals with you two around than any other time before."

"Yeah, true," Chester said, looking deep into my eyes, "but did anyone die?"

I looked around the room, as if searching for the answer, "No, I suppose that you're right. I'll put up with you two if you can keep on delivering on that one."

"We have been while you've been putting your feet up."

Lawrence's dry sense of humour was something that I had forgotten, but immediately knew that I would need to up my game if I was to continue competing with him. But it wasn't just me that he was after.

"You weren't the only one who fancied a little lie down, Sergeant Ellis. Young Earnshaw over here tripped over a twig and spent three weeks in hospital."

Earnshaw, who was standing beside a mirror, glancing at himself sideways, immediately burned a furious red colour, one that had been so permanently etched upon his skin in recent weeks that it seemed like his face had changed dramatically.

Earnshaw was not having his prestige attacked so soon after my arrival, "Two weeks I've had to put up with this! They've been non-stop!"

I could do nothing but chuckle along with everyone else, which only made him more furious.

"I'll have you know, it was all quite serious, I could have—"

"Could have died?" interrupted Hamilton, his square shaped head jumping up and down as he laughed.

"Oh, don't you start..."

"More holes than a sieve this bloke!" Hamilton suddenly exploded, as he threw his head back at his own joke. I wondered for how many weeks he had been sitting on that one, just waiting for the perfect opportunity to let it out of the bag. He had timed it perfectly as what he had said, coupled with the bright red face of Earnshaw, sent us all over the edge.

"Yeah, well...you can laugh! But most of the poor blokes in there for longer than two weeks are put down, like a horse. It means I'm made of stronger stuff."

"How on earth do you come up with this rubbish?!" screeched Lawrence, as he cajoled Earnshaw, trying to get him to see the funny side.

We giggled and tittered for a few more minutes, before someone produced a pack of playing cards and we all sat down together, just like old times. It was going to be easier to win a game now that McKay wasn't around.

For all the laughter and joviality, the hole that he had left was a sizeable one, despite the quietness of the young boy in person. He was a shy figure in the group, but one that could always be found and talked to, which was why I was going to miss him immensely. It was one thing to miss him while I was on the other side of the channel, but now that I was back where he should be, it was far worse.

"Andrew."

Captain Arnold took me by complete surprise, somehow silently sneaking into the room whereas before he would have made a far grander entrance.

He looked different to how I had remembered him.

He had always been tall, and he still was, however, his shoulders had gradually edged forwards to the point where it must have taken a good inch or two off his overall height.

His face too had thinned out dramatically and he had allowed a few hairs to begin to stick out from his chin in the form of stubble, which he would not have been seen dead with a few weeks before.

He held out his hand, which I shook emphatically. It really was great to see him, despite the fact that the eyes that had once burned with enthusiasm seemed to be nothing more than embers nowadays.

"It's good to see you, Sir."

"You too, Andrew. Now tell me, what have you been up to?"

"I'll give you one chance at guessing, Sir. And it doesn't involve lying on a beach."

*Had he really wanted me to answer that question? There really did seem to be something wrong with him. What a stupid question to have asked a man so recently out of hospital.*

**4**

------

"I bet you feel right at home here, don't you Hamilton?"

"How do you mean, Harry?"

"You know," scoffed Earnshaw, looking around him dramatically, "this sort of place. I bet it's what you're used to."

"Not exactly, no. I've got rather accustomed to that ghastly little room, listening to your snores every night of the week."

Each of us let a slight chuckle pass over our lips.

"The kid's learning," quipped Sergeant Lawrence. "Only dish it out if you can receive it back, Earnshaw."

"I'll bear it in mind, Sergeant."

Earnshaw had been larking around, but I was almost certain that there was a chance that Hamilton had frequented this kind of room on a daily basis.

All around us seemed to be the epitome of luxury,

from the highly decorative walls, right the way down to an ancient looking drinks cabinet in the corner of the room. There seemed to be paper and files almost everywhere I looked, more often than not accompanied by a well annotated map or three.

Even the men that skulked around here, looking down their elongated noses at us, seemed to have a much better looking and more well fitted uniform than the one that we had had chucked in our direction. Everything in this world seemed to be far different from the one that we had just come from.

Everything was so clean and highbrow, that I bet even the Captain, whose father was a Baron, was beginning to feel rather out of place. I was sure that he was regretting the decision to have forgone a shave once again, the stubble that stuck from his chin almost dripping the grease onto the highly polished floor at his feet.

There was no doubt in our minds, this one was going to be a briefing like no other. That was if it was a briefing at all.

"I reckon it's to tell you you're all up on a charge of treason," remarked Lawrence as we journeyed to the immaculate room.

"Oh yeah? Then why are you two delinquents coming with us?" retorted a flustered looking Earnshaw.

Lawrence shrugged, "I suppose someone has to escort you to the cells."

The worried look on Earnshaw's face deepened, until we were ushered in to the grandest room that we had seen in our lives. We were half expecting the King to suddenly stumble in, accompanied by the men of the Order of the Garter. At the sight of the room, we all knew that we weren't to be arrested, at least not in the conventional way.

"Gentlemen," announced a boisterous and flamboyant general as he strode into the room. Our chairs shot back what felt like several feet as we all cannoned to attention, pulling our bodies into the tightest and straightest position that they had been in months.

I had never been in the presence of such a high-ranking officer as this one before.

"As you were. As you were," he took up a chair on the other side of the great desk that we sat in front of, as he cleared a space before him so that he could rest his hands upon it.

"I'm General Palmer. Shortly we will be joined by some others, that have a great deal of information to share with you. But before they arrive, I would like to express my own personal gratitude and appreciation for everything that you have carried out so far. It has been most impressive."

"Thank you, Sir," mumbled Captain Arnold, as if he was awestruck to be in the presence of such a great man. I wondered if he was envious of the General's great moustache. It really was a sight to behold.

The moustache danced around excitedly as

General Palmer's great, booming voice erupted once more.

"Ah, yes, come in. Do come in. Gentlemen," he announced, turning to us as he rose from his chair. "May I introduce you all to Majors Symonds and Hillier."

Both the figures emerged from the floor-to-ceiling door, arrogantly striding in and snapping to attention. General Palmer barely even batted an eyelid.

"Hugh, George, this is Captain Arnold and his men."

We looked each other up and down, before the tone changed, and we started to get down to business. I noticed that one of them, either Hugh or George, was keeping a very close eye on his brown leather brief-case, which matched the gleaming tall boots that he had pulled on over his feet.

"Okay then chaps. You obviously know that you are here for a job that we would like you to carry out for us. It is of the utmost secrecy and so we would like it to stay that way for the time being. Hugh."

The briefcase-less man got up, before fiddling with one of the General's annotated maps.

"Two nights ago, we received a message from one of our informers on the other side of the line about a possible attack. Unfortunately, the informant who supplied us the message was compromised and so it has been incredibly difficult for us to verify why she thought an attack was imminent."

"She?" queried Lawrence, the Major seemingly taking offence at the foreign accent that spat towards him.

"Yes, Sergeant. She." The Major looked slightly frustrated but carried on regardless. "Our informer, for whatever reason, was convinced that there was a gas attack imminent. One that was clearly being prepared for weeks in advance.

"We think that, if this is the case, that the gas that the Germans are likely to be deploying will be held in small, steel canisters. Akin almost to a four-two shell. However, we aren't sure."

"Where do we slot into this, Sir?"

"Well, as we are unable to verify the information with any of our contacts, we want you to head over there and take a look for us. We estimate that if an attack is likely to occur, then the provisions would have already been moved up into the frontline."

We looked at one another, warily, all of us with a thousand and one questions, but it was only the Captain who managed to voice even one.

"And if we do see these canisters, Sir, what are we to do with them?"

General Palmer interrupted, "Destroy them if you can. But, if the attack is to take place on the scale that our contact suggests, then you probably won't even make a dent in their reserves. This is primarily an identification and verification operation. Hopefully, you won't even have to discharge your weapon."

*Hopefully.*

I never had liked that word all that much.

"Unfortunately," spoke Hugh, "there is not much that we can do on a preventative level. The attack is more than likely going to happen. We just need to know so that we can…reduce the potential casualties."

"You mean choose which men are going to be coughing their lungs up?" Earnshaw would never have fitted in too well with these circles.

"Of sorts, yes."

"You will go tonight, gentlemen. You will have the rest of today to familiarise yourselves with the maps and what limited intelligence we have on the German's use of gas."

"Tonight?" I suddenly found myself blurting, "Why so soon? We would need more time than that to acquaint ourselves with the intelligence."

"I'm sorry, it must be tonight. The wind direction begins to change at around midday tomorrow. If you can destroy some of those receptacles tonight, then we have a chance of using the Germans' own gas against them. Anything after that and we risk an attack without taking the necessary precautions. I'm sure you understand?"

His eyebrow, as bushy and over the top as his moustache, raised itself in my direction.

"Yes, Sir. Perfectly understood, Sir."

"Jolly good. Anything else, Hugh?"

"Yes, Sir."

He began tugging around at a large and well-detailed map, which he proceeded to explain to us about our point of insertion and where the canisters were likely to be located. Together, we came up with a plan of where to go in and where it would be best to withdraw from, given the terrain and situation out in No Man's Land.

"I propose to withdraw around here," announced Captain Arnold, thumping a muddied finger down on the map. "There is a bombed-out farm house there that we can potentially use as cover."

"Very well, that fits in with where we want you to go."

"So, that's all agreed then? We go in here," he thumped the map once more. "Scout around here. Pick up a prisoner if possible. Withdraw to the farmhouse to interrogate for further intelligence, before falling back to our frontline."

"Sounds perfect to us," Hugh announced, looking towards George and the General. Each of them seemed equally impressed. George had still not uttered a word but had continued to clutch to the shiny briefcase under his left arm.

"What do we do with the prisoner, Sir? Once we've got what we can from him?"

"It is up to you, gentlemen. Whatever the situation dictates. But one thing must be made clear, he does not, *does not,* make it back to his own lines. Is that clear?"

It was, crystal.

We all knew already what the situation would

dictate. It would be difficult enough to extract six British troops, who may or may not be injured, never mind a tag-along German who would spend the remainder of the war in a cell more comfortable than McKay's own.

The situation would dictate that he would not make it back to either lines.

I already felt sorry for the poor bloke, and we hadn't even met him yet.

"One thing that is imperative to ascertain from the prisoner, as it will determine all of our precautions," Hugh looked us all in the eye, determinedly. "We must find out what gas it is the Germans are preparing to use."

"Major Symonds is right. We simply must find that out at all costs. Whatever it takes, gentlemen. Unfortunately, our contact was not able to let us know what it was. I am sure she would have told us if she had known."

There was something about this informer that had me transfixed. Maybe it was the mystery that had surrounded her, the no-named, faceless woman who had decided our next operation for us. I wondered if she even knew that we were going to take action against it.

My mind fantasised about all the other wonderful bits of intelligence that she had gleaned since the war had begun, and how she was desperately trying to end all of this so that we could go home. A plethora of questions began to dance their way through my mind;

Had this been her first time? How had she come across the information? How did she get it to the British?

All of these wild meanderings roamed around the barren moors of my mind for a few minutes more, before I began to think what might have happened to her. I wondered if she had been chased through villages and side streets, or if she had got away with much more ease and elegance.

As I pondered all of these things, there was something that was attracting me to her. Maybe it was the way that we now had this operation to have in common. But I soon settled that it was something far deeper than that.

Had she felt as trapped in her corner as I had done in mine?

I wasn't sure.

There was just something that we had in common. Something more than just the operational circumstances that we now shared.

"Now, there is, as always, the possibility that things might begin to go a bit haywire. In which case, some splendidly clever chaps have been developing these for you."

Major Hillier suddenly found his voice, except it did not seem like his. It was far deeper and rumbling than I had been expecting, far more baritone than it should have been for such a frail and weak looking stature that the man possessed.

"These are black veil respirators. If one of the canisters is destroyed, whether deliberately or accidentally, attach one of these under the nose and over the mouth and breathe as normal."

From his precious briefcase, he produced a small envelope sized piece of cloth, which he handed to us individually, keeping one for himself.

"You remove this tab here, place the pad over your nose like this. And tie the cloth behind your neck in this manner."

I wasn't sure who the "splendidly clever chaps" were that the General had referred to, but I wanted to meet them immediately.

*Surely, they could have come up with something better than that.*

"You've got to be kidding me," muttered Lawrence, "that's all the protection we get?"

"It's the best we have," grumbled the General, "besides, it's far better than relieving yourself into a handkerchief!"

His moustache doubled over in the same manner as the rest of his body, as he guffawed in the most exuberant of manners.

*It's okay for you. You're not the one that's going to be putting them to the test.*

We spent a few more minutes in each other's company, before General Palmer dismissed us back to our quarters.

As we left the room, I caught the voice of Captain Arnold, slipping in a few words to the General before we left the grandeur of his office.

"Sir, you are aware that we have a court martial

among us tomorrow? Is there really no one else that can take our place?"

"Well aware, my boy. Don't you worry, you'll still be able to give evidence when you make it back."

*If we make it back.*

## 5

There was far more to the room than I had expected and at first, I was unsure of whether I had been shown into the right place or not.

I had expected it to be cold and damp, the heavy air clinging to my chest in the same way as if I was to place my head over a pan of boiling water. I had anticipated grey and solemn walls, accompanied by an equally depressing concrete floor, with no source of light other than a meagre candle.

But the room was surprisingly pleasant, the walls a plain white in colour, with no signs of what it had been used for in the last few weeks. There was a bed to one side, which looked far more comfortable than the one that I had been used to sleeping in back in Britain. The covers looked far less itchy for one thing.

The issue of the light was resolved by the rectangular window at the top of the wall, not big enough for the occupant to peer out of, but large enough for the natural light to come streaming through in abundance.

All in all, the room looked almost quite cheery, with a bucket of clean water sitting in the corner, ready for its occupant to give himself a rinse over, or maybe even take a sip from.

The room, however, was lit up by the owner of the basic accommodation, a cheery grin settling optimistically on his face.

"Not a bad little place you've got yourself here, McKay."

He looked up at me, almost proud of his own little space, the only time he had not had to share a room with other men in a good many months.

"Good, isn't it? Cheap too."

He chuckled, as he pulled himself a chair that had been slid under the desk in the corner, as he beckoned me to sit on the edge of his bed.

I was right, it was more comfortable than that hospital bed.

I noticed that the hand he had gestured to me with was now the home to a set of battered and chewed up fingernails, a side effect, I assumed, of the long and nervous wait that he had been condemned to endure ever since he had got out of the hospital.

"Thank you for writing to me," he said, eventually, lifting up his hand to have another go at the nails.

"You wrote first. It was only out of a sense of duty."

"It was more than that, you missed me."

I smiled.

"You doing okay? They treating you properly?"

"I never thought prison could be like this. You know, it's actually kind of okay. I wake up, sit around for a bit thinking, maybe write a letter or two and then go back to sleep. Not a shell or bullet in sight."

"That's good."

"Food isn't too bad either, better than what Earnshaw can come up with, anyway."

"That's not saying much."

He laughed again. It was strange to see him so happy, particularly after the way I had seen him in the last few weeks. It was almost like being caught out, and now paying the price for what he had done, had somehow set him free. He now seemed like a normal young lad again. He seemed jubilant.

"The lads who look after me are decent enough too, for policemen."

I suddenly found myself at a loss for words, as I thought about the possibility that this was the last time that I would ever see him again.

"How are you? The scars, can I see them?"

"Do you really want to?"

He nodded.

Warily, I unbuckled my trousers and rolled up the woollen pants to my thigh, so that he could have a look at my war wound. He took a look at the tender and enflamed scar that now ran up from just above my knee, by three or four inches, the only sign that I had that I had once had a knife shoved into me.

"That looks sore, mate. I'm surprised they let you out so soon."

"Oh, they didn't. Not really," I said, redressing myself, "I kind of insisted. Didn't want them lot to be without me for any longer than necessary."

"What makes you think that they needed you?" joked McKay.

"Have you met them?"

He laughed again, weaker this time.

"What went through your head, when they got you?"

I was slightly taken aback by his question and the sudden change of tone to the conversation. In all honesty, I could not remember, in fact I was almost certain that not a lot was apparent in my mind, other than the ghoulish figure of Bob Sargent as he stood atop the sniper's dugout.

"You lot," I lied. "I thought of you lot if you didn't have me. I was certain that you'd end up in all sorts of trouble if I died."

"Hasn't done me much good," he joked, looking around him, but I could see the hurt that was in his eyes. "Want to know what I thought about? Our conversation, in the Canadian's hidey hole. You know the one I mean?"

I knew only too well, as it still haunted me in my darkest moments. McKay had asked me about death, the certainty that every soldier on the Wester Front faced, but not one that was frequently discussed, nor even considered.

"Yes, I remember."

"Well, I've had a change of heart. As I was lying there, blood coming from somewhere, I began to think that maybe death isn't all that bad. And it was while that thought went through my head, that I concluded that there must be something else. Something after this life, I mean."

I looked away from him for a moment, choosing instead to look at the lonely bucket in the corner. It was only at that moment that I realised what it was really for, and he certainly wasn't going to be washing in its contents anytime soon, that was certain.

When I looked back up at him, his eyes were all glazed over, with a sparkle to them that is only apparent in a man who is trying with all his might to hold back his tears.

"I like to think that maybe there is something after all this. I don't know what, but there must be something. It really would be nice to see my family again. So that I can explain what happened."

"You don't need to, Fritz. We know why you did what you did. You don't need to justify yourself."

He sniffled, "But the people around them won't know that, will they? They won't understand."

"Have you managed to write to them?" I asked, trying to move the subject along somewhat.

He shook his head, trying to simultaneously shake the build up of tears away.

"Can't face it. I didn't know what to say. It makes me feel bad for all the months where I haven't written to them, I reckon it would just be better if they think I am dead already, you know?"

A bolt of guilt suddenly struck me directly in the heart, as I thought of my own family and all the many months where I hadn't written to them, to at least let them know that I was alive. I had only written to my sister while I had been lying in a hospital bed, she had barely crossed my thoughts since I had got back to France.

*Maybe I should try and write to her soon.*

"I'm looking forward to it though, Andrew."

I looked at him, slightly confused.

"To find out what it is on the other side. I'm not scared of it at all now. It is what I deserve, after all. Thank you for everything that you have done for me, I know that you have tried everything that you possibly could have done to get me out. The Captain too. But I need you to know that if it is a firing squad that I am to face, then I am more than ready. I've been preparing myself for it for a while now."

The tremor that was so frequent in my hand was now not quivering my limbs, but inside my own mind, it was shaken all over the place. What he had just said had hit me and hit me hard.

I knew McKay better than anyone else that I had met, and I had thought that I had wanted him to escape a firing squad, if at all possible. But, hearing his own admission that he was ready, a troubling thought began to impress itself upon my heart.

*I want you to die too, McKay.*

It tormented me greatly, as I only wanted what was best for him, which was the fulfilment of his own wishes. But, at the same time, I knew that McKay had become a distraction, a figure that I always had to keep an eye on. Like a son to me.

If I was to allow him to keep getting in the way of my thoughts, then there was a very real possibility that he would get me killed, and I still wasn't quite ready for that fact just yet. Maybe I would be soon.

It wasn't the first time that I had wanted one of my best friends dead. I had thought it too of Bob Sargent. And look how that one had ended up.

I still blamed him for the four-inch scar just above my knee and the stiffness in my joints that I woke up with in the middle of the night.

*You shouldn't think like that. Get him out.*

"How are all the others? Are the faring well?"

I pulled myself together. He had done it, so should I.

"Yeah...they're good, all raring to go now."

He sat bolt upright in his chair, before leaning forwards, just glancing at the door to make sure no one was going to burst through at any second.

"Yeah? You have a job?"

I felt guilty almost immediately, a part of me reserving just a slight element of pride that I was still a free man. It was at that moment that I realised how much I was looking forward to going back. Before, I had felt like I wanted to be back with the men and that was all I needed, but now, I realised, that what I wanted more than anything in the world, was to go back over the wire.

I wanted to be out on a trench raid again.

"Sorry, McKay. You know I can't tell you."

"Oh, go on. I could be dead in forty-eight hours."

"But you might not be."

"Either way, what am I going to do with the information? Give it to the Germans?"

He regretted his joke as soon as it tumbled from his mouth. It was in bad taste.

"Fair enough," he conceded, observing the unrelenting look on my face.

I glanced down at my wristwatch.

"Look, I better be off. I said I'd be back about an hour ago."

"Got any smokes?" he interrupted as I got up to leave. "Please? They only give me ten a day. You know that's nowhere near enough for me, don't you?"

He continued to bite his fingernails in the slight gaps in his speech, as if that had taken over from his old habit of smoking every minute of every day. If he kept that up, he would have no nails left by the end of the week. If he was allowed to live that long.

"Please," he begged, "for old times' sake?"

I took a swift look at the door and back towards the short, efficient fighter that I had come to love. I was sure that he could have powered his way out of the cell, if he had really put his mind to it.

"Okay. But then I have really got to go."

"Got any cards?" he whispered gently, through a mouthful of saliva.

"For old times' sake?" I asked, as I watched the first few tears roll down his cheeks.

"Maybe some other time, eh?"

"Some other time, McKay. As soon as we see each other again."

"Goodbye, Andrew."

"Goodbye, McKay."

## 6

It felt good to get back to the others as we all started preparing ourselves for our latest excursion. I had needed to get away from McKay and I found myself trying to forget about him as best as I could.

I had to accept the fact that he was now a dead man and that, in all likelihood, I would probably never see him again.

He had started to make me think about my own mortality, which in turn had made me think of home. My sister in particular, was the one face that I could not seem to shake, a disappointed expression the one that she would adopt when she laid eyes on the fateful telegram. She would have been expecting me to write. I had found it so easy to when I was still in Britain, the hospital bed the perfect place to ponder what to get down onto the paper.

But as soon as I had exited the ward for the final time, nothing would come out. It wasn't that I didn't want to write to her, but it was putting into words what it was I did night after night, and how I dealt with myself. I could not pretend to be the boy that she knew, when I had done so much and seen far worse while I had been in France.

Even if it was the most mundane of letters about the weather, I decided that I simply must write to her the minute that I got back.

*If I get back.*

Chances were, I would have one less person to write to anyway, as McKay would almost certainly be dead. His court martial was due to start first thing in the morning. I could almost picture the presiding officer dusting off his black cap as we prepared ourselves for the night ahead.

I looked up from my kit for a moment, taking the opportunity to light my final cigarette from the pack that I had shared with McKay. Earnshaw was standing over a bowl of water, gently dabbing away at his face and making sure he looked as spotless as possible.

I saw no point in the enterprise whatsoever, in an hour or two he would be coating himself in burnt cork anyway. He had really started to make a right fuss over the way that he looked in the last couple of days.

He did it, he claimed, so that he could come across as attractive as possible to the opposite sex, as he never knew when he might meet the woman he was meant to spend the rest of his life with. But then again, as Lawrence had taken great joy in pointing out, even one night might be enough for the rest of a trench raider's life.

"What you doing putting that stupid thing on for?" barked Lawrence from the far side of the room.

"It's for good luck," announced Earnshaw, as he twiddled a gold ring, forcing it to the base of his finger.

"I haven't seen you wearing it before," commented Chester, as he sidled up next to Sergeant Lawrence, the two Canadians uniting themselves against Earnshaw.

"So what? I think it's lucky, so I'm wearing it."

He flexed his hand out in front of him, trying to admire it in the best light possible.

"Why have you bought so many rings anyway, Harry?" asked Hamilton, politely.

Earnshaw scowled, "I've always bought them. They're an investment. For my family. I want them to have something to show for my life rather than a meagre army pension when I'm gone. This way, they'll get everything that I earned."

He had become fairly materialistic in recent weeks, making a fortune on as many card games as he possibly could, before spending the cash the minute that he got it, once even buying the ring off the man that he had just defeated, paying well over the odds in the process.

He seemed to only care about accumulating as much material wealth as he possibly could.

Gone were the days where he sourced things for people, before selling them on at an extortionate profit. He cared little for that anymore, instead trying to have as many possessions to his name by the time he donned his wooden jacket.

His change of tack played to my advantage, as he had more or less been the sole supplier of my paraffin, which meant that not only did I not have a hip flask to put it in anymore, but I had lost my source of the hideous liquid as well.

"I don't know how you get your hands on some of the stuff you do. It has to be stolen, doesn't it? Did you used to be a bit of a dealer back on civvy street, Earnshaw?"

Earnshaw quickly shied away from the mirror in front of him, slipping the ring from his finger and shoving it in the darkest pit of his trouser pocket.

"Why don't you leave me alone? Pick on 'im, he's more worthy of your ridicule," he flicked a hand towards Hamilton. Lawrence barely took another breath.

"What about it, posh boy? Why are you here anyway when you could be three hundred miles behind the line?"

Hamilton just blinked at him, clearly frustrated but not willing to take the bait.

"What kind of a name is Hamilton anyway? Hardly a name for a Lord such as yourself is it? A bit common, I think."

Hamilton's face flashed a vibrant shade of red, he was trying hard to ignore it, but it was proving too much for him. I let Lawrence continue to goad every-one, more because it was done in jest and without any real malice, but also because it would get everyone's blood boiling, it would get them in the mood to kill.

"Yeah, far too common. I don't think you're from that realm anyway. You've made it all up. Father in the Admiralty? You must be joking! I don't think you even *knew* your father, did you?"

Hamilton exploded, most uncharacteristically, "That's where you're wrong!"

"About what? Your father or your common name?"

"Both! I suppose..." his voice trailed off in a whisper, as if he was ashamed of what might come out of his mouth next. Silently, Lawrence pressed him.

"Hamilton *is* a common name...but my father is in the Admiralty. His name is not Hamilton."

"So, he did leave you?"

"No! Not at all! If anything, I left him!"

I was intrigued now, as was everyone else in the room, including Captain Arnold who had been a silent observer until now.

"How do you mean, Hamilton?" interrupted the Captain, as he hoisted himself upright on his bed.

"It's not my name," he grumbled, ashamedly finding a chair to plonk down in to, his head following into the palms of his hands. "David Hamilton is not my real name."

"Say that again, one more time," babbled Lawrence, who was getting so excited that his voice climbed two or three octaves.

"I stole someone else's name. To get away from my father. I joined up without him knowing. That's how I haven't been recalled yet. He's probably been looking for me for ages."

"Hamilton," I said, not really knowing how else to address him, "I don't quite follow. Why would you change your name? What is your real name?"

"My real name is Geoffrey Lymes. David Hamilton is the name of my housemaid's son. She was not a well woman and he wanted at least another year with her if he could. I offered to take his place, at least until the whole thing unravelled. That way he got a bit longer with her before she passed away."

We all sat for a moment, completely dumb-founded. No one spoke but sat with eyes squinted as we tried to get our heads around what it was that he had said.

"So, you're telling me," muttered Earnshaw, "that you're out here, pretending to be this Hamilton bloke, while he's back at home out hunting with your mates?"

"It's not exactly like that, but you're on the right lines."

"I've heard it all now," gasped Lawrence, as he flopped out onto his bed. "You Brits are crazy."

I couldn't quite believe it. The square-chinned, straight as a die, Anglican boy who had broken almost all the rules in the book, just so he could come and fight. I couldn't help but feel slightly proud of him, which manifested as a slight smirk and chuckle on my lips.

"So, you do like to break the rules every now and then, Hamilton? Can I still call you that?" teased

Chester, as he began to fumble around with his kit once more. I found everyone in the room quite remarkable. We continued to almost die alongside one another on a frequent basis and yet, there was still so many secrets still lurking in the darkest corners, only coming to the surface when we least expected it to.

"Yes, as long as the pretence continues. And yes, I suppose I do."

"So, who is it that doesn't like to smoke then?" I teased, "Hamilton or Lymes?"

He thought about it for a moment, "Come to think of it, the real David Hamilton never seemed to stop smoking."

I held out a new carton for him, which he proudly took. He got used to the feeling of it in his mouth for a moment, before I lit it.

I had barely ignited the end before he was coughing and spluttering every ounce of mucus that he could muster. His face immediately burned the brightest shade of red that I had ever seen before. After what seemed like several minutes of coughing, he pushed the cigarette towards me.

"Turns out that David Hamilton doesn't like smoking either anymore," he staggered around the room, trying to find a glass of water or anything that might help him recover.

After we had all calmed down and once Hamilton had resumed his normal breathing pattern, Captain Arnold decided that we had had enough fun.

"Right then, boys. Try and get some sleep. We have

four hours till we need to move to the front. Make the most of it."

Like obedient orphans, we did as we had been told, but I was certain that not one of us got any sleep. I know that I didn't.

My head was swimming with thoughts and ideas, of McKay, my sister and everything else in between. But there was one thought that recurred far more than any of the others, the one that had been bugging me for hours.

*The informant. What did we have in common?*

I could not for the life of me work out why I had become so attached to her, when I knew so little about her. All I knew was that she had been an informer, who had made a dash for it shortly after providing the British with the information about the gas attack. Other than that, I knew nothing.

*There must be something. There must be some reason why I feel closer to her.*

I began to doubt myself, about whether I had a common ground with her, or that it was just the fact that she was a woman that I had felt attached.

Maybe it was because I imagined her as my own sister, the one that I had started to think of more the closer that I got to death. There was some truth in it, my sister was the only female face that I could recall at the moment and I must have spent hours staring at the ceiling as I saw her racing through the streets of France, the Germans hot on her heels.

I hoped she had got away.

I knew that my sister was safe however, she was three hundred miles away in Southampton.

As I thought about her, running through France and then Southampton, I double checked that I had my most valuable possession on me. They would certainly be coming with me tonight.

Once, it had been the hip flask, with its foul demonic liquid sloshing around inside that I had to depend on. But now, it was the letters that sat just above my heart that would become my talisman.

Maybe I will write to her, just the minute I get back.

*If I get back.*

## 7

I had been relishing the chance to get back out and over the wire to be able to fight. But the moment I had put my foot on the bottom of the trench ladder, all thoughts of relief and happiness went out of the window.

Dread and fear firmly took their place in my guts. I could feel my insides tightening, as if they were tensing up and hardening themselves for a bullet or another knife to find its way through my body.

I had not thought it until now, but this was the first time that I was going to be heading out without the hip flask. I needed it. I needed to at least feel it on my person.

*GRHMN.*

No, it was gone. It was all down to luck now and I wasn't quite sure if I was deserving of a share of the portion.

I wanted nothing more, as we scurried our way

across No Man's Land like a colony of rats, than to be back in my bunk, where I felt relatively safe and secure.

*Crack.*

My body jolted, as if the round had passed through my skin somehow.

I froze.

It took me far too long to work out that the rifle crack had been a long way off, the bullet meant for someone else entirely. It could have even been an accidental discharge. But I had been away from this life for long enough to be lulled into a sense of security, into a reality where things like that do not happen. I had started to jump at every noise, every artillery shell that landed, every flare that fizzled, all because I had become so accustomed to the noiseless hospital ward, where screaming nightmares was the worst that it got.

I tried to distract myself as best as I could, to get my mind off how inadequate I was feeling. I didn't want to be the one responsible for any more deaths, if I could help it. I wanted all of them to survive tonight.

I looked around in the dark, hopeful of seeing a face or two that might reassure me and so that I could reassure them. I knew that I wasn't going to be able to keep them all alive and, even if I tried my utmost, there was a chance that I would merely put more people in danger by trying to save one person alone.

That was where my weakness now lay. Previously, I had not really cared for anyone, particularly not myself, but now I cared too much, to the point where I would gladly put other people's lives in danger just to get one person out alive.

I had become scared myself, about death, as I laid prone in that hospital bed back in Britain. The thought of it now terrified me. I did not want to die. I was only nineteen years of age. No one deserved to die that young.

I had remembered the advice of my very first Sergeant, George Needs, who had given me the hip flask many months ago now.

*You must lose your hope. You will die here.*

My hope was well and truly gone, but the fear of dying, the one that had been masked so excellently by the copious amounts of paraffin, had started to seep through strongly, the quiver in my mind growing more and more tremulous by the day.

The ground was cool, so cool in fact that it felt almost quite damp, as I felt large clumps of dirt beginning to stick to me and come along for the journey across No Man's Land.

I felt comfortable with the way in which we crouched and ducked as we made our way through the dirt and debris to get to the Boche wire. Everyone that I was out with on that night, had been out with me before, and had proven themselves capable of avoiding detection. There was no cause for concern there.

Similarly, there was no reason to doubt the advance party who had been sent ahead of us some twenty minutes before. They had ventured out in much the same manner as we had done, approaching the German wire, before stopping and waiting.

We waited for the perfect time to go in, where the noise around us was at a minimum, where we could guess at how many enemy soldiers were in a trench.

The advance party however, waited at the wire for as much noise as possible, a quick volley of artillery to be exact, just behind the German lines, so that they could cut the barbed wire freely.

It was a risky business, waiting for the shells to scream directly overhead. All it would take would be one, slightly defective shell and there could have been four dead British soldiers waiting for us at the wire, rather than the gaping wound in the German frontline that we were met with.

They had done an excellent job. As always.

I wished that I knew who they were, so that I could thank them. Maybe they could see us right now, as we lay quite still, ensuring that we had not been spotted on our approach.

We hadn't.

It was time for us to go in.

The wire had been cut at the end of one of the fire bays, where the traversing trench ended and led on to another fire bay. It was best for us to try and slither in here if we could, for the Germans left the darkest corners of their trench alone, and so were less likely to see the spectral figures slithering into their trench uninvited.

It was also where General Palmer and his men had

suspected that the canisters, if they even existed, would be located.

The four cold and damp corpses that lay in wait right above the German's head, began to grow impatient with him, as he seemed determined to thwart our attempts to destroy their plans of attack. I heard the strike of a match, the accompanying smell of the burning stick slowly fading into the night, to be replaced by the stench of tobacco.

I hoped that Hamilton would not start choking at the smell.

It felt good to have just the four of us waiting for the German to move. It was just me, Captain Arnold, Earnshaw and Hamilton lying on our stomachs. Lawrence and Chester were further back, at the ruined farmhouse, waiting to cover our backs as we scarpered from an exploding enemy line.

It was not that I did not trust them, I had no choice but to, but it was the fact that they had not been able to prove themselves close up, not in my eyes anyway. They were snipers, long-distance killers, men who had not been in amongst a vicious and demanding hand-to-hand battle with the enemy.

And there was also the small matter of the huge scar that bubbled down the side of Sergeant Lawrence's face. He had remained particularly coy over the matter, but there was something between him and Chester, that told me there was more to it than some kind of childhood accident. The scar still looked tender, it was recent.

It was for that reason, that I was glad that it was the four trench raiders, not the snipers, who were preparing to enter the trench.

Eventually, the German began to move along the trench, at least his cigarette smoke did, which was the only signal that we needed. I made out the blackened face of the Captain, as he looked back at us all and gave us a curt nod.

*Here we go. Back into the fray.*

We took it in turns to slide down into the trench, my spiked truncheon and revolver sliding around in my sweating palms. I hit the floor, with a soft thud, before moving away to the other side of the trench to make way for the incoming men.

I bumped into the Captain. I stayed there, my face pressed into the back of his neck, while I felt Hamilton do exactly the same behind me. It was a calculated move, one that allowed us to group together and stay in the shadows until we knew that everyone was accounted for.

We waited for an age before Earnshaw joined the queue.

Hamilton lightly tapped me on my right arm, which I passed along to Captain Arnold. It was time for us to go.

There was very little light for us to go by as we stumbled along the trench, treading on the outsides of our boots so as to cut down on the noise that we would generate. It was inevitable that they would hear us coming eventually, but we hoped by then it would be far too late for them to do anything about it.

The singular source of light was from a very weak looking candle, that looked so pathetic I almost began to feel sorry for it. But it was just enough to hide our true identity while also affording us some guidance in the unfamiliar surroundings.

We moved along the trench as one body, sauntering past the sleeping soldiers who lay head to toe on the fire step. From what I could see, there was three of them there. We would leave Hamilton and Earnshaw to stand over them, to wait for their time to strike. They would need to be quick, ruthless, this all needed to be carried out with a frightful efficiency.

There was one sentry up ahead who stood atop the fire step, from what I could see from behind the Captain's tall, statuesque figure, his cigarette chucking up a stream of smoke as he thudded along the trench. I thought I could hear him humming. Maybe that would help us.

As we approached the end of the fire bay, where the man was stood on watch, he started to turn, which was when the Captain spoke.

"*Alles in Ordnung?*"

He had been practicing his pronunciation over and over where, to my untrained ear, he sounded almost as naturalised as the Kaiser himself.

The German stood confused for half a second, as he tried to mumble out some sort of response to who he could only assume was a superior officer.

"*Erm...Ja...*"

His confused, stuttering response were the last words that he would ever speak, as Captain Arnold elegantly hopped up onto the fire step with him, as if he was about to take a look at the British lines, before a knife found itself embedded in the man's chest.

He let out a low moan, as if he was merely being deflated, as the Captain began to twist and turn the knife so that it made a catastrophic wound.

As if he was some sort of a long-lost friend, the German threw himself on the Captain, who gradually helped him down from the fire step, and propped him up in a sitting position, as if he was just tired of standing. The man had no desires to make anymore noise, as he focused wholeheartedly on managing to get enough oxygen into his punctured lungs.

I heard the knives behind me withdraw and I knew immediately that the sleeping soldiers would never be waking up.

All of a sudden, a darkened shadow appeared at the end of the trench, as if he was a ghost who had mystically descended, to keep a watch on us.

As quickly as he had appeared, my mind began to fill in the blanks. The body slowly became enlightened, to reveal the khaki green coloured uniform, covered in a smattering of blood.

The body was small and compact, with a wiry frame that looked almost unable to support itself. The hair was blonde and floppy, so greasy that it was a much darker pigment than it should have been.

But then I saw the face, baby-like and innocent, devoid of anything truly remarkable, but a handsome face, nonetheless.

It was Bob Sargent.

He looked at me for a moment, tilting his head over to one side, as if he was inspecting my soul.

*Why are you here? I thought I had got rid of you.*

As the body turned and tried to run, I caught sight of the uniform once again. It hadn't been khaki, it was a steely grey, the most depressing of colours known to man.

I hadn't imagined the figure. I had imagined the face.

Immediately, I gave chase, my bones cracking louder than the footsteps that echoed across the whole of the Western Front.

The man had barely even made it to the end of the fire bay before he came within my arm's reach.

*Clump.*

I felt one of the sawn-down nails get stuck in the shoulder of the man, which proved difficult to withdraw, especially as he fell to the ground. Some of his blood sprayed over me as I withdrew, knowing with a certainty that I was going to have to do it again to make sure this man kept quiet.

I closed my eyes and did what was necessary. The love of killing and maiming was never truly apparent in my heart, but it was even less so as I made sure that the German sentry would never get up again.

Bloodied and battered, I pulled him up onto the

fire step, to let him sleep next to his two other compatriots.

"You alright?" whispered Hamilton, into my mind, as I sucked in air so furiously that I thought I might be the best defence mechanism against the gas attack.

I felt sick. Why had he been there? Why had he appeared in just the same way as he had done when I had shot him a few months ago?

I had got rid of the paraffin, that was what was causing all those hallucinations.

*Wasn't it?*

Or maybe Bob truly was haunting me. Maybe he really did want to see me dead.

All I knew was that it had happened, and I would have to try with every ounce of my mental energy to block him out from returning.

Otherwise, I would be joining him on the other side of the mortal realm.

# 8

We all stared at one another for a few moments, as if no one really knew what to do next. I glared vigorously at Captain Arnold, willing him to speak, to do something other than just stand there and look at the body count that we had just created.

The bags under his eyes seemed to loom larger and darker than they had done before, so prominent were they on his face that the darkness of the dugout seemed to create a cave-like impression on them. He still had not had the motivation to have a shave, which meant that the stubble on his face was slowly coating itself in a layer of grease and grime, that would start to smell in a day or two.

It was as if he had lost every desire to look presentable, a worrying trait for a man who had previously been so immaculate in his appearance.

I was used to his unmoving stares by now, more often than not looking like he was engaging his brain to think about what to do next. But, in that moment, there was nothing, the dying embers behind his eyes a window to his mind, as if he was completely empty on the inside.

It was like he had lost every motivation to even command us. We all stood watching him, to tell us what to do next, but without the nudge from one of us, he would have quite happily have stayed stood there for the remainder of the night, I was quite sure of it.

He had always been so certain about why he was fighting in this war, instead of taking up a desk job that his father so easily could have sorted for him. But now, ever since the McKay situation had been found out by the other officers, he had become a changed man, one who was clearly conflicted about why this war was being fought.

I too had had the same reservations. Why was it that we were fighting against this evil enemy, and yet our own officers were prepared to line one of our own up against a wall to be shot?

It was a question that I desperately needed answering, but now was not the time, there were far better places to question those kinds of moral implications rather than the German frontline.

"Sir?" I whispered, coaxing him from yet another of his trances. He blinked profusely, as if he was trying to get a speck of dirt out of his eye, or maybe to wash away the tears that had taken him by surprise.

His body jolted as if a current of electricity had shot through him from head to foot.

"Sir? We should move into the dugouts. Carry out the next phase of the plan?"

He said nothing, but vaguely nodded in my direction, not looking in my eyes but choosing instead to let his gaze soar right over the top of my head.

I immediately spun on my heel, leaving Captain Arnold to fend for himself, he was more or less completely useless to us at the moment and I hoped the alone time would be enough for him to pull himself together again. I had been able to do it, so why couldn't he?

I pulled Earnshaw and Hamilton in towards me, pointing to the fabric flap of the dugout. We had to hope that there was at least one man in there, ready to be taken prisoner, but not too many that we would be overrun.

"That dugout there. I'll grab a prisoner, you two deal with anyone else in there. Got it?"

They nodded, which filled me with an overwhelming sense of achievement and exhilaration. I finally felt like I was back where I belonged.

There was nothing pretty about what we were about to do, there was only one way that we could carry it out. We needed to be hard and fast, take everyone inside by surprise. That way, even if we were faced with ten men, then we could at least deal with a few of them before they pulled themselves together and worked out what was happening.

It was not an exact science, but we would have to make do.

Earnshaw had his eyes closed, which was odd, as I never had him down as a praying man. In fact, he was the only one of us in the whole team who seemed to have no faith in anything apart from himself. Maybe that was who he was praying to as he clamped his eyes closed. Or it could just be because he was dreaming of something much further away than this.

I tapped him on the top of his arm with my revolver, which awoke him and made him realise that now was certainly not the time to go into himself, especially as Captain Arnold had already reserved that space for himself.

Hamilton's eyes on the other hand were wide and raring to go, as if he had just awoken from one of those most refreshing of sleeps, ready to face what was ahead. His face, although covered in grease and cork, was one that had not changed in the slightest since he had been with us. I thought maybe that it was because he had not been with us for as long, but then realised it had been the same amount of time that I had been in the team before I got hooked on the paraffin.

Apart from a single puff on a cigarette, Hamilton had not changed in the slightest.

"Ready?"

I was, so I expected them to be as well.

I would go in first and nab the first figure that I saw. There would be no time for analysis, no questioning who I thought might have the most information or the easiest one to crack, although that would have been nice, there was simply no time.

A single shout from one of the occupants would be all that it took for the world to come crashing down all around us.

Hamilton stood poised over the fabric curtain. There was a faint flickering candle inside, weaker even than the one that had been outside, I guessed.

The curtain was pulled back. I stepped in.

There were no shouts of recognition of an enemy soldier, no bellows to attract the attention of everyone else, just a series of grunts and gasps as we did what we needed to do.

I tried to imagine what it would have been like for those men, quietly lying on their beds, waiting for their watch, or reading a book at the table in the centre of the small room, only to be suddenly interrupted. I tried to guess what the fear was like in their body, as three towering figures dramatically flew into the room, their faces hidden under layer upon layer of blackness. Their eyes would almost certainly gravitate towards the weapons that we brought with us, the truncheons, revolvers and knives that was the extent of our arsenal.

They would know who we were immediately. But before too long, it wouldn't matter, as they would more than likely be dead.

I rushed over to the first figure that I could make out, just sitting up in his bed, writing a love letter to his sweetheart or a poem for his mother.

He looked up at me, his spectacles the size of two pocket watches, quite carelessly and as if he had been expecting us this whole time. His face was quite round in shape but at the same time gaunt looking, as if his cheekbones would slice my skin if I was to run my finger along them.

His face was, however, a kind one, which made what I was about to do all the more difficult.

I heard the final few gasps of the dead men just bounce off the walls of the room, as Hamilton and Earnshaw dispatched of the other men who were snoozing in their beds.

For some, unknown reason, my eyes had been drawn to the man who was on the far side of the dugout, which meant I had two or three more strides than the other two to do before I got to him. It was plenty of time to pull my fist backwards, as if drawing a bow ready to release the arrow.

As I charged at him, I simultaneously swung my arm around and forwards, smashing into the weak resistance of his nose as I did so. Blood sprayed everywhere, predominantly from his face, but also from my knuckle.

His spectacles hit the floor, as did the pencil that he had been using to pen his love notes. His head bounced around for a few moments, before the second blow really delivered the message to him.

"English? You speak English?"

"Yes," came the babbling reply, as he fought with the blood that had gushed to his mouth.

Good. That was the only criteria that we needed.

"You're coming with us. Up. Up."

"Come on, get *up*," emphasised Hamilton, gripping

him under his arm and practically yanking him from his bed.

"My glasses...I need them...I need to see where I am going."

I threw them towards him, before he shakily placed them back on the bridge of his bloodied nose, wincing pathetically as he did so.

I almost felt like apologising to him for a moment, the blows that I had delivered quite clearly awfully discomforting him, to the point where I thought he might cry.

"What is happening? What are you doing?"

"Shut up or I'll put a bullet in you," Earnshaw's prayers seemed to have worked. He was back to normal.

"Harry, grab the Captain. We're falling back, as per the plan."

"Got it."

As if the German soldier had trained with us, we moved effortlessly towards the trench, before forcing him up his own trench ladder.

We would now head back to the ruined farmhouse where, hopefully, both Chester and Lawrence were perched waiting for us, like a nervous mother. Our rifles would be there too, if they hadn't run off with them.

The farmhouse was completely void of anything that might have distinguished it from any other piece of rubble out in No Man's Land. There was no structure to it or form, just a series of half-walls that still defiantly stood at around shoulder height if I was to stand up straight.

It was a perfect bit of cover for what we needed it for, a quick interrogation out in the field, before heading back home. Once there, I would hopefully begin to feel safer, as it was one step closer to home.

However, the height with which the walls stood was also a major disadvantage, as it was the only thing that could offer some real cover from enemy bullets. As such, it was the ideal target for a salvo of artillery, or for a machine gun to begin sweeping through. It would also be the first place that a patrol would look for a missing soldier.

But it would have to do. Hopefully, if we were quick enough, we would be on our way back to our lines before they even realised that the oversized-spectacled German was missing.

"Thanks for waiting for us," I muttered at Lawrence as we stumbled into the stone walls of the farmhouse.

"We're more loyal than you give us credit for, Andrew," he said, handing me a rifle. I checked that it was made ready by pulling the bolt back and having a feel for the brass round inside, before I focused on anything else.

"Blimey, what have you done to him?" grunted Chester, harshly, as he scrabbled over to the German.

"Sergeant Ellis gave him a whack on the nose, Chester. Some Germans need a little physical persuasion. It's not easy when you're not just looking at them through your sights," Earnshaw was feeling fired up and I could tell that he was yearning for some sort of a scrap.

"I'm not on about that," Chester said, rebuking Earnshaw, "I'm talking about *that*."

It was only at that moment, in the dim light of the French midnight, that I realised what it was he was on about.

The scarlet liquid had left some sort of a trail right the way through the rubble that we now occupied, until it started to pool around the German's leg.

"My leg," he said, wincing like he had done when he had replaced his spectacles. "I got it caught in the wire. I ripped it out of me."

"Right, let me take a look at it," announced Chester, beginning to lift the leg up to some light.

"Not yet," Captain Arnold rasped stubbornly. "We need to talk to him first, then we decide what we do with him."

It seemed like the situation dictated that we were to behave like animals.

## 9

"My name is Captain Arnold."

The Captain knelt down in front of the German and spoke slowly and clearly, succeeding in patronising the young man before him, whether it was intentional or not, I did not know.

"He speaks perfect English, Sir."

He looked to our new prisoner for confirmation.

"My name is Unteroffizer Franck Maas, Royal Bavarian, Twelfth Infantry Regiment. What do you want with me? To kill me?"

He seemed scared, which was not surprising considering the situation that he now found himself in. I was not sure that I would be reacting as calmly in his position.

"No...No..." the Captain sighed, pulling his woollen hat from his head, revealing the hair that was becoming just as greasy as the stubble on his chin. His voice trembled slightly, as if he was not even convincing himself of the fact that the German would remain safe.

Maas could detect the uncertainty in his voice.

"What are you going to do to me? Why have we stopped here?"

They were all fair questions, as one would assume that now we had a prisoner we would keep on going until we made it back to our line. The young bespectacled German would not get the answers that he was craving, only a distorted variation of an answer from the Captain.

"We are not taking you back to our lines. There will be no record of you ever being in our care. Do you understand what that means?"

The German began to look around fearfully, his eyes wide and tearful behind the thick sheets of glass.

He began to whisper something under his breath in German, which seemed to have the rhythm and feel of a prayer to it, but I could not understand a word that he was saying. It was at that moment, as a wave of cool air brushed over my skin, that I realised that we needed McKay. He was the only one of us who could actually speak any German.

I looked up briefly, at which point I caught Chester's eye and I got the distinct impression that his gaze had been burning at the side of my cheek for a considerable amount of time. We locked eyes for two or three seconds, before he turned away again, to man his post and scour the route that we had just come down.

*What had I done wrong?*

Had he noticed something about me? Maybe he was harbouring the same doubts about simply sitting here and waiting for a helping of artillery, especially without the luck of the hip flask. He seemed to hate me, for whatever reason, but I could not for the life of me work out what I had done to scorn him.

*None of that matters right now. The German at your feet does.*

"*Ja...Ja...Ich verstehe...*I understand. I am here so that you can kill me if I do not do as you say."

"You're a fast learner."

I caught the eye of Lawrence this time, who seemed to be staring at me in exactly the same way as Chester had been. I tried to push them from my mind for a moment, they would call me out if there was anything that would be endangering anyone's life and, right then, that was all I could care about.

"We want to know about the attack."

Lawrence looked back out across No Man's Land as the Captain started to interrogate our prisoner. Maybe that was it. They were getting twitchy about being out here. They felt threatened. They felt like the war was about to come to them, it could get personal at any second.

There was something under the surface that was making these two imperceptibly nervous, the only reason I had picked up on it was because of their apprehensive glances.

Something was causing those fears, those glares.

And I suddenly became adamant that I would find out as soon as I could, hopefully before we all got ourselves killed.

"What attack? I don't know anything about an attack?"

"We know that there is an attack planned. We have valuable intelligence that tells us it is correct."

Maas began to get panicked, flustered, as he began to rub at his cheeks in desperation.

"What attack? I know nothing of any attack! Don't you think we would have known if an offensive was planned?"

"Oi, keep your voice down," chirped Earnshaw, giving the German a slight prod with the barrel of his revolver. "We don't want your chums over there coming for us. You know what will happen if that happens, don't you?"

The German held his palms up in submission, "I'm sorry, I'm sorry. Now please take that thing away from me."

"Does he mean you or the revolver, Earnshaw?"

The Captain shot him a dirty look. Now was not the time to be reigniting another playful feud. Earnshaw smirked at him like the elder brother who had just got his younger sibling in heaps of trouble.

"Look," explained Maas, his heavily accented and crackled voice bubbling out into the Captain's face. "I do not know anything about an attack. I would have told you if I did. What have I got to lose now? You have guns on my head."

Captain Arnold glanced up at me, looking for some sort of a hint on what to do next or some guidance. The initial questions had been vague, as we didn't want the man to just go along with anything that we had said. It is basic human instinct to tell your captors what they want to hear.

I pursed my lips and sucked my cheeks in, he knew straight away what my advice would be. We would need to get specific, gradually at first, but slowly drip feed him information until he could confirm or deny what we thought was the case.

After that, if he didn't give us anything but the naivety card that he had played so far, we would have to get nasty. That was going to be difficult, seeing as the German that we had managed to pick up looked like everyone's younger brother.

I was sure that Lawrence would have no issue with knocking him around a bit, however. He seemed like that sort.

# 10

"Honestly, I do not know anything about what you are on about. Please, you must believe me."

I looked across to Captain Arnold, whose face was telling me the exact same thing that was flashing across my mind. We didn't believe him in the slightest. It seemed like the more he tried to protest his innocence, the more we became convinced that he knew exactly what we wanted to know.

All he had to do was just spill the beans and then all of this would be over for him. He might even be able to make it back to the German lines before anyone realised that he had gone missing.

Everyone, particularly our two Canadian friends, were growing impatient with Maas, who seemed so defiant that I thought we would be better off returning to get ourselves a new prisoner. This one did not seem to be the right one for what we needed him for.

He could tell that we were getting irate, which only spurred him on further to defend himself, telling us various tid bits of information that we knew to be true already.

"When an attack is imminent, we are told about twelve hours before. Our officers are given maps and information on your lines to help prepare themselves. If you were to attack on one of those nights, imagine the amount of information you would be able to gather."

"Hamilton," said the Captain, "grab a rifle and go up on watch with Lawrence and Chester."

"Yes, Sir."

Maas seemed quite offended that his little speech had been all but ignored by Captain Arnold. In response, he simply sat and stared at his hands, muttering the same old prayer that he had mumbled a few minutes before.

But, this time, I could make out individual words, their harsh and dirty-sounding syllables resembling something like a throat clearing or someone who was quite unwell.

With all the words that I could hear, not one of them seemed to be 'God' and so I found it quite difficult to ascertain as to who it was he was praying to.

I could sense both Lawrence's and Chester's eyes burning into my skull, their gaze one of irritability and annoyance.

I looked up at them.

"We need to get a move on here gents. This isn't one of your tea parties. We're still a long way from safety out here."

"Yes, thank you Sergeant."

Arnold's voice was just as highly strung as Lawrence's, the air around us suddenly becoming thinner as everyone's throats tightened somewhat. I didn't like where this was going. We were all beginning to turn on one another, the longer that we stayed in the ruined farmhouse.

The Canadian was right, we would need to do something, and soon, whether that was releasing the German, disposing of him, or taking him back to our own lines with us.

The rest of the German army were going to discover the dugout soon enough, at which point I was sure there would be a thousand flares up in the sky, replaced by the howling hell hounds of the German artillery.

Captain Arnold had started to blink rapidly, again like he was trying to forbid the tears from streaming down his cheeks.

He was a broken man, a damaged officer, who wanted nothing more than this whole war to be one elaborate nightmare. He stood in silence for what felt like minutes, the embers that glowed behind his eyes slowly dwindling, as if someone had gradually poured on a cup of water.

Someone else was going to have to step up once

again, someone else was going to have to make the decision that could quite easily result in seven dead bodies in a ruined farmhouse.

I wondered for how much longer the distant stares were going to be, not just tonight, but every night. I wasn't sure if this was now what he was going to be like, every time he came up against something that might threaten his mind, that he simply shut down and gave up.

That was not the officer that had been leading me for the last few months. I felt partly to blame all of a sudden, as if my months of drinking and bickering with Bob had been a factor in his mental demise. It could well have been.

But there was nothing I could do about that now. It was all in the past, even if it had been something that had affected him.

As the one who felt partly responsible for his mental stutter, I began to take charge. I started to make decisions on his behalf.

There was no more time to be messing around. I pulled out my revolver and pressed it into his head.

I thought I could almost see Lawrence dancing a merry jig on the spot at the sight of what I was doing. Things were about to get messy, which was just the way the barbaric Canadian liked it.

"Franck. We *know* that there is an attack coming. We *know*. Do you get what I am trying to say to you?"

He tried to look up at me, but I kept his head

pointing down towards the ground with the solid steel of my Webley.

"But...but—"

"We know that there is a gas attack coming. We know that it is imminent. Probably at some point over the next twenty-four hours. You are going to tell us the rest. If you don't, we will leave you here. You will die slowly."

I manoeuvred the revolver so it was pointing straight at his groin, the one place in the world that no soldier ever wants to get hit.

He got the message.

"The gas attack...oh...yes. It is happening. Soon."

"When?"

"Tomorrow."

"Be more specific."

"I don't know."

The barrel found itself pressing into his skin, so forcibly that it would be reasonable if the skin started to break and blood began dripping from it.

"I do not know! I do not know!"

He spat and coughed as he tried his hardest to vehemently deny the allegations of the revolver, whilst simultaneously trying his best to keep his voice to a minimum.

"How did you...how did you know?" he whimpered pathetically, as I released some of the pressure on the side of his head in sympathy.

I toyed with the idea of leaving him in the lurch but thought better of it. We would all be better off if we were able to keep him onside and get as much information from him as possible.

But first, I would play with him, just a little bit. To remind him who was in control, nothing else, no strange sense of satisfaction could be drawn from this.

Still, the Captain remained silent.

"We know that in all likelihood the gas is in canisters. Those canisters will be deployed to your frontline very soon. What we want to know is when are they likely to release the stuff and, more importantly, what it is that is actually in those canisters."

He looked up at me again, his eyes seeming to mumble the prayer just as much as his mouth did. Eventually, as he started to dribble from his mouth, but also his eyes, he began to speak in a language that I could understand.

"Please...tell me...how did you know? How did you find out?"

I let his question linger for a few moments, as I felt several pairs of eyes suddenly lock themselves on me, as if I was the only one who knew the answer.

"Please..." he repeated.

I looked to the Captain. That was one step too far, one that I was not willing to take without his blessing. Surprisingly, he weakly nodded in my direction. I hoped that was a sign that he would be resuming command as soon as possible. It was not something that I was ever especially comfortable with.

"Our intelligence services found out."

"But, *how?*"

"They had a source. She managed to get a message out to her contacts before your lot began to track her down."

He looked at me and began trying to get to his feet. Instinctively, I took a step backwards. I pulled the pistol away from him and let it dangle down at my side. He may have been an enemy soldier, but he was of no real threat to me right now.

He removed his spectacles, and, for the first time, I realised that he had the most wonderful blue eyes that I had ever seen before. They were as vibrant as the hottest summer day, the only clouds that were apparent were the ones that were soon rolling down his cheeks as he continued to beg for more information.

"Please...please...do you know if she is okay?"

I tried to not let my face give away the true answer, but instead tried to manipulate his thoughts to work in my favour. If he thought that there was a possibility that she was still alive, then maybe he would give something to us in return. Maybe this nurse meant something to him, reminded him of his sister maybe.

"The gas attack. What is it and when?"

He swallowed what must have been a football-sized blob of saliva, as it looked as though it had taken every ounce of energy to be able to force it down his throat, but eventually, he spoke.

"The Kaiser Wilhelm Society."

I looked around at the others for anything that

resembled any recognition from our briefing earlier on. But there was nothing.

"What?"

"The Kaiser Wilhelm Society."

"What is that?"

"It was inscribed on the crates. All of the crates that carried the canisters."

"Go on."

"We weren't told directly about what was going to happen, but it did not take a genius to work out what it was they are planning. A gas attack, a big one I think they are hoping for. Somewhere in this sector. I do not think they have decided where yet."

"What makes you say that?"

"They issued us with these masks. Just a ball of cotton really, that is to be dipped in a solution as soon as the attack starts. To protect us. I have friends, many of them up and down the line who have also been issued the same. Some of them are fifty or sixty kilometres north of here. There is no way that they have enough canisters to have them all the way up the line."

"The canisters, what was written on them. Is there anything more you remember about them?"

"*Ja,* one other thing. Just one word under The Kaiser Wilhelm Society."

"What was it?" I was growing incredibly impatient, as it increasingly felt as though he was biding his time, just waiting for the moment that his comrades swept in and took him off into the night sky.

"*Chlor.*"

"What?"

"*Chlor.* I think you call it chlorine?"

"Chlorine? But that can kill a man, can't it?"

"I would guess that is the proposed outcome, Earnshaw," I retorted, turning my attention back to the German.

"The girl, the one who passed the information onto you, is she okay? Did she make it out alive?"

I stared him down for a moment, trying to work out exactly why he had taken just as much of an interest in the invisible woman as I had. Maybe he really did picture her as his sister.

He continued to have no luck with me and so turned to the Captain to petition him instead.

"Sir? Please tell me if she is okay?"

The Captain shrugged, mercilessly.

"What makes you think we know? We only get told the bare minimum."

The German sank back to his knees, this time unashamedly grovelling at the feet of Captain Arnold.

"Take me with you! Please! She'll be trying to get to England. Take me with you, send me there, at least that way I might find her again!"

"How would you know that?"

"The girl, your source, that was my Emilie. She is my girlfriend, my sweetheart. She was a nurse at the hospital. We always said that if something like this was to happen, she would try to get to England. She wrote me a letter. She was alive three days ago."

I felt sorry for him all of a sudden, the rage that I

had felt for him just a few moments ago at his stubbornness completely wiped from my conscious mind.

"Please…" he begged as he began to weep again, "Please take me with you…"

I looked across at Captain Arnold.

*What is the situation dictating here?*

## 11

The artillery that suddenly screamed all around us was utterly terrifying. I hated every second of them, even if they were from our own guns, as I didn't trust them. I hated the lack of control that I had over them as soon as they began to rain down.

In a firefight there was always something that I could be doing; firing my weapon, reloading or issuing an order to someone, but in an artillery barrage, I could do nothing but sit and wait for the lucky shell that would fall on my position.

I would probably be able to see it coming, that was the worst bit. A small black dot, I supposed, that began to give up and plummet to the earth, gradually growing larger as it filled my vision. There would be no hope in trying to outrun or outmanoeuvre it. I would be dead before I could think about what I was trying to do.

*All I can do is tuck myself in and hope.*

The air felt as though it was full to bursting with metal, both complete shells and the more tormenting fragments of shells already burst. The ground that I tried to bury myself into trembled as if it was having some sort of a seizure.

We had scurried across No Man's Land like rats, but as the shells fell all around us, I wished that we had been able to dig ourselves into the ground like rats also.

The deep and throaty roar of the explosions never seemed to cease for what felt like an eternity. I looked at my wristwatch, that was two minutes of shells so far. They would surely have to stop soon.

I wondered how many guns were firing at us and whether the shells that fell just behind the farmhouse were intentional, or if their aim was off. I thought for a moment that it was at first to scare us, before the rounds began to chase us back to our lines, but I was not so sure.

A huge cloud of dirt began to drift over the top of the farmhouse, depositing a strange dust over every one of the inhabitants. The cloud continued to roll as the shells did not let the earth settle for a single second, as it continued to shake the dust around in my own head for a while after the barrage had stopped.

The ringing in my ears banged away for many more minutes after the cessation of the rounds, where the only sense that was really worth anything was my eyesight, and even that was hindered by the dark cloud that engulfed us.

Still, Lawrence, Chester and Hamilton continued to keep watch over No Man's Land, however ineffective it might have been.

As the ringing in my head slowly began to subside and in the ensuing silence that followed, I allowed myself a brief respite, to think of something far better than sitting in the ruined farmhouse.

I did something that I had rarely done before, unless I had known I was in a relative safety.

I thought of home.

For some peculiar reason, I saw thinking of home while out on a raid one of the greatest signs of weakness that I could think of. It made a man more sensitive, compassionate even as he thought about the happy days gone by of walking through fields and streets that were calm and cheerful.

Except this time, I did not think of my family, but of the life that I had enjoyed before I was tainted by the experiences of war. It felt strange to me to think of it, so distant in my memory that it felt more like a utopia than anything that resembled a reality.

There was a time, I thought, where an artillery shell did not fall around you. There was a time when you did not have to carry a rifle around with you for your every waking moment, or watch as a friend slowly died. There was a time, not so long ago, where I had not taken another man's life.

My gaze drifted over to the German, who had pressed himself up against the sturdiest wall that he could find, as if a direct hit would somehow be repelled by it.

I began to feel sorry for him, for the way in which that he too had been taken from his previous life, trained to kill and then ripped from the only thing that he still had some control of; his own letter writing. I wondered if it was the nurse that he had been scribbling to as we dragged him out, or if he had already known that she was on her way to England. Maybe she had already managed to get a note to him.

I thought about them for a while, about how they had met and developed together, all the while the pulls of the girl seemingly growing stronger to me.

*There was something that we shared. But I could not work it out.*

I checked myself over for any holes or drips that would indicate that I was wounded in any way, but, thankfully, there was none.

As I patted myself down, I gave my own brain a mental slapping.

*Don't make him human. He is still the enemy.*

"Right then, we've got what we came for. Let's make our way back?" Lawrence was itching to get going, I had never seen him so nervous. For a moment, it looked as though the scar that lined the side of his face was bulging in anticipation of what might happen next.

Captain Arnold had needed a good shake up, which is what he had received courtesy of the artillery shells.

"No. That's not what is going to happen. I want to head back, locate some of the canisters and destroy them. Maybe bring one back for our chaps to take a look at."

Lawrence pulled his rifle from the top of the wall and slid his back down it, furious with the Captain.

"You have got to be joking. You can't seriously be suggesting that we go back and risk all of our lives for that stuff?"

"You didn't go there in the first place, Lawrence. You were sitting in here, remember?" Earnshaw couldn't help himself but get a swipe in. He was ignored by everyone.

"*If* we do make it into those trenches alive and that is a big *if* of itself, then how many do you think we can destroy?" He looked to the German, "How far apart are they?"

The German gave it some consideration, "Right now? Probably one every three or four fire bays. Depends how long you want to be in there. But you made decent work of my friends."

"So, we could maybe get three or four canisters. Is that worth it for all of our lives? They have hundreds, if not thousands more canisters, up and down the line. If we were to take three out here, it's hardly going to save the world, is it?"

"I am the one that is in command here, Sergeant Lawrence. If that is what I order you to do, I expect you to do it."

Lawrence fell into a silence that was filled only by

the tension that was stretching through the farmhouse quicker than anything I had ever experienced before. All it would take would be one match strike for the whole thing to erupt in a ball of flames.

"Sir," I whispered, turning my head away from Lawrence so that he would not hear what it was I was saying, "with all due respect, I do think it would be futile to head back. The Germans would almost certainly have found out about our presence now. They would be on a much higher alert. We would be almost guaranteeing the loss of one of us if we were to go back."

He thought about it for a few moments before Hamilton chucked in his tuppence worth.

"I think we should go. If we can bring back one for our boys to analyse, think of the good that it would do. Besides, if we do release some of their gas, the Germans would be the victims to their own weapon. It might even make—"

"Shh, quiet."

It was Chester, who had twitched just enough to get his words out. I noticed too that Hamilton's body had stiffened somewhat to react to whatever it was that had made Chester speak up.

"What is it?" queried Captain Arnold, as Lawrence sprang back up into his rightful place.

Hamilton took his place by sliding down the wall and crawling over to us.

"We're going to have to put that discussion on hold, Captain. We are going to have much bigger problems.

There was some sort of movement up ahead. Just ahead and over to our left. It has stopped for the time being. I'm not sure what it was."

It could have reasonably only been one thing; a patrol of enemy soldiers. Whatever their intentions were, there was a good chance that things could get quite heated, which had made Sergeant Lawrence's scar begin to sweat far more than he did from his hairline. He was nervous. We all were.

The Captain pulled the German into his face by the scruff of his shirt, "What could it be?"

"How should I know? I am not in the lines anymore. I have no knowledge of what is going on in there, just like you."

"Could it be an offensive?"

Maas simply shrugged. He had become indignant towards us, as if he knew that his best option was to be found by his comrades, rather than just left in the dirt with a hole in the side of his head.

The Captain practically dropped Maas back on his backside, as he scurried over towards Lawrence, on his hands and knees.

"Keep an eye on him, Earnshaw."

I wasn't entirely sure what he expected him to do. I thought it quite unlikely that he was about to make a break for it, he was in just as much of a precarious position as we were.

I accompanied the Captain up towards an opening in the ruins, which must have been a doorway at some stage of its life, as the others took up a position behind the meagre wall that would barely offer up protection against a raindrop, never mind a bullet.

I narrowed my eyes, as I tried to filter out the final clouds of dust that was still failing to settle after the artillery had sounded. I could see nothing out of the ordinary, not for No Man's Land anyway.

The ground all around was uneven and threatening, with remnants of trench life littered everywhere; old, rusting barbed wire, trench duckboards and I was sure that I could even see a gas light sitting on top of one of the smashed trees.

Of course, the obligatory corpses were there, too plentiful to count. But I could not make out any of them moving.

"Where are we looking?"

"That way, at your eleven o'clock. There was just one wide mass. Like a wall coming towards us. Then it disappeared. I think it dropped into a shell hole."

"And you're sure you saw something?"

"We both saw it, Sir," protested Chester. "There was definitely something moving."

The German cleared his throat. We all jumped.

"Quiet."

"You do not want to know what I have to say?"

"Say it."

"Only if you give me your word that you will take me back with you, there is no point in me going back to my own lines now. I will most likely be executed if they found out what I had told you."

"You're going to tell us anyway, mate. Otherwise none of us will be going back to our lines."

"I want your word."

The Captain lost it, scurrying over to the German and whipping his revolver out simultaneously. The noise that he generated in doing so was enough to attract the attention of even the deafest of enemy soldiers.

"You *are* going to tell us anyway. Or I'll put one of these in the side of your head."

The German pursed his lips for a second, debating whether it would be better to call the Captain's bluff or not. In the end, he realised that he had no more bargaining power, we had already got what we had wanted from him. He was worth little to us now.

"They will be coming to clear up after the artillery," his weak and crackled voice spoke as he tried to control the tremble in the back of his throat. "They will be very mad that you had been in our lines. The artillery was to try and stop your retreat so that they could catch up with you. Finish you off themselves."

"Who's *they?*"

He toyed with the Captain for half a second more, enjoying immensely the small amount of power that he suddenly seemed to have. He had captivated us all.

Then, just one word came from his lips. One that we all recognised and feared immensely.

"*Sturmtruppen.*"

*Stormtroopers.*

## 12

I had always wondered what I was going to think about when my time to die was nearly upon me, but it still surprised me nonetheless that I was thinking of my family once again. It was more the guilt over the fact that I still had not written that letter to my sister, the one that I had been promising myself to write ever since I had walked out of the front door of the family home.

If I was to be truthful with myself, it was more because I had absolutely nothing to say to her anymore. How could I tell her about what I had been doing since I had returned when she more than likely simply wanted to know that I was safe? In all likelihood whatever it was that I really wanted to say would simply be erased by the serial censors that my letter would have to pass through, before being allowed on its way.

I thought that the whole thing seemed ever so

slightly pointless. But still, I should at least write to let her know that I was still alive.

*You'll have to start writing soon. Otherwise it will be too late.*

I tried to refocus my mind on the situation at hand, as I had begun to drift off in my attention, which was incredibly dangerous, considering the predicament that we were in.

We could try and make a dash for our lines before they got to us, which might result in a hot pursuit that would end up with us riddled with holes from bullets on both sides. It was still a possibility, but one that I knew was dwindling the longer that we left it to try and identify the shadows.

"Over there, movement."

It was Hamilton who had spotted them, his crystal-clear diction working wonders to my battered and assaulted eardrums. I followed his finger, hoping that what it was he pointed at was much further away than it was.

*Blimey. They're getting close.*

They moved slowly, as one large mass, crouching and crawling into shell holes and behind bits of debris every now and then. At this rate, they would be on top of us in less than a minute. We needed to deal with them, and quickly.

Lawrence and Chester suddenly began to squirm around in their places, their rifles twitching as if they were as nervous as their handlers.

"How many of them are there? I can't see. I can't

tell." Lawrence was getting agitated, the sweat dripped from his hairline now beginning to wash away the heavy layers of black that he had plastered all over himself. He was really nervous.

*What had happened to him before? Where had the knife wound come from?*

"Calm down, Lawrence. Be quiet. Just stay still."

I was glad that Captain Arnold had somehow relocated his marbles, now asserting the authority that had been expected of him in the first place. It wasn't just the orders that we craved but the physical presence, the one where we could feel him standing there with his shoulders upright and chest puffed out. His confidence rubbed off on us all.

Still, no one seemed to know what to do, despite the vicarious confidence that we had all benefitted from. Not even the Captain seemed to have any ideas. But he quickly locked himself in his own mind again, trying to recall anything from history that he possibly could that might help him in the slightest.

He would need to work quickly, as we really did not have long at all until we would be surrounded.

"What do we do?" asked Lawrence, apprehensively.

He was beginning to frustrate me, a seasoned Sergeant who should have known better than to put the wind up the younger and less experienced men around him.

"Should we take them? I have one that I could take now," rasped Chester, excitedly. These two boys really wanted the fight to be over and done with before it was on their doorstep. But it was simply not feasible now. We were going to have to think of something else.

The only thing that I could think of was engaging the enemy troops, while one man alone tried to make his way back to the British line. We had all of the information that had been requested of us, but if all of us were to perish in the farmhouse then the whole thing would have been futile.

If only one man made it back, then we could turn this defeat into something of a success.

But I could see that Captain Arnold had different ideas about what we were going to do. As always, he wanted to stand his ground and fight. In his eyes, we were still far away from completing what it was we had set out to achieve. He still wanted to get back in their line and steal a canister, before it was too late.

He had a strange and uneasy optimism about him.

The German cleared his throat once again, making us all jump in unison. I was surprised to see that he was now perched at the wall, without a weapon, but otherwise adopting exactly the same position as his enemies had done.

"You should use me as bait. They will come if they know that I am here. That way you can have them all in one place. It will make it easier for you. You will likely make it home that way."

We all stared at him in complete disbelief for a few seconds, no one said anything.

"Maybe not home," he said, his trembling voice

correcting himself, "but safety, at the very least. That is what you want isn't it?"

We looked at one another, for perhaps a little too long, trying to read one another's minds, before I realised that we had advancing enemy troops directly ahead of us. I checked my gaze and refocused on the darkness in front of me. I could see no movement for the time being.

"Why are you helping us to kill your countrymen?"

He shrugged, "I do not care for them. There is only one person that I care about right now. And she is on her way to England. Please...take me with you."

I did not know what to make of his proposal, as to me at least, he seemed quite slimy, as if he was the kind of person that would merely agree with the person who was pointing the biggest gun at his head. And, if that turned out to be the German patrol on its way to introduce themselves to us, then we would very much be in even more serious trouble than before.

"What do you think?" Captain Arnold whispered across to me.

"It is an option, Sir. It is one of the only ones that means we'll be able to get back relatively safely...It does mean taking him back with us though."

"Not necessarily," he said coldly, making sure that the German had got the message.

*Any funny business and you're just another corpse.*

"We can't trust him, surely," muttered Lawrence, his compatriot seemingly in complete agreement with him.

"He seemed sincere about this girl, Sir. If he remembers that we are the only ones that can help him get to England, then I'm sure he'll play along."

The Captain gave it a brief thought, "You do realise that you will be arrested as soon as you get into our lines? You will spend the rest of the war in a prison camp?"

"But at least I will be safe. I will be one step closer to finding her again."

There was an uneasy silence, where all of the conflicting views suddenly began to clash in the air above the Captain's head. It all fell on his shoulders to make the call, whatever he said, we would do. But I was still ever so slightly concerned that, in his mind, we weren't finished yet. He was still trying to find a way of getting back to the enemy frontline.

Eventually, he must have thought better of it.

"Okay," he grumbled. "Okay. You have a deal. But we will kill you the moment we get wind of anything that isn't as we agreed. Understood?"

"Yes, Captain."

"So...what do you suggest?"

Maas began to shuffle around, as if he was about to retell a story that his mother had relayed to him years ago. He was finally beginning to enjoy himself.

"Leave me in here, towards the rear of this building and let me call out to them. I will say that I am wounded and was left here by you lot. All you have to do is let them come in to get me and then wipe them out the minute they're all inside."

"What do you reckon?"

I did not like the way that Captain Arnold was continually asking me of my opinion, as in truth, I did not have one. I did not have a clue as to what to add to this discussion. Neither, it seemed, did anyone else.

I shrugged, "I don't see any other way out. They know we're here. We're going to have to tackle them eventually. Might as well be on our own terms."

"It means that we won't be able to go back into their lines."

"That is your call, Sir."

There was a slight delay, "Okay, let's do it. Let's set it up. Lawrence you keep watch out front. Keep your head down. And you," he pointed accusingly at Maas, "I'll be standing right here, the first round is reserved for your head if I get a whiff of anything off."

"What is a whiff?"

"Everyone else, in the corners. Stay still. We do this as quietly as we can. Revolvers only if absolutely necessary."

I watched as Maas began to drag himself across the ground, before propping himself up on the smallest wall possible, that once upon a time must have stood proudly at least eight feet tall. As he winced and pulled himself around, I caught a few syllables of his prayer-like whisper once again.

*"Für dich, mein Geliebter...für dich..."*

I did not understand a word that he was saying, but it did not sound like he was praying to any God, but to someone who meant far more to him than anything that I could understand.

The girl must have meant an awful lot to him, as I watched him grab the gaping wound that had opened up on his lower leg from his own barbed wire, before squeezing it on either side, so much that I thought he would pass out.

The blood spilled out faster than if he had upended a bucket of water, before he practically collapsed into the wall as he released his skin. Blood had gushed all around him, leaving a far greater amount than he had needed to.

I looked across in the darkness towards the Captain, who was standing there, as equally dumbfounded and full of admiration.

*At least he was committed.*

Hopefully that was a sign of things to come. Hopefully he was on our side now. *Hopefully.*

My eyes fell on Hamilton, who was already staring at me, as if he was trying to tell me something from the other side of the ruins.

I put my thumb up towards him and mouthed "You okay?"

He stared at me, statuesque for a moment and just as I was about to move over to him to check up on him, I got a trembling nod of the head. He didn't look all that convinced with himself.

He was a good soldier, but I wasn't sure if he actually knew it or not. He was a hard worker, one that always wanted to know answers to his newfound questions and to adapt to whatever situation he was in.

He possessed a courage that I thought was unequalled by any man that was currently with us, superseded only by McKay, who was now paying the price for a slight anomaly in his bravery.

I thought about his father for a few seconds and wondered if it was really true that he did not know where his son was. I was sure that a man of his standing would work out that his housemaid's son had still not signed up and would start to ask questions.

How long could a housemaid's son last against the interrogation of a man of such high stature?

Maybe he was proud of his boy, the one that had been so desperate to join up that he had joined the ranks, where he knew he would see a decent amount of the action. But, then again, surely a father would want his son to survive as long as possible, in which case there would have been no way that he would have joined our team. His father couldn't have had a clue.

I hoped he did find out soon enough, as I wanted Hamilton to be recalled by his father. I had started to like him far too much to see him dead under my jurisdiction.

"Maas. Now. Do it."

He nodded, before calling out.

*"Hilfe. Bitte hilf mir...Hilfe..."*

## 13

Maas continued to call out to his comrades, but I had no knowledge of whether or not they were responding to him at all. Maybe they had direct orders to ignore such a call and go straight after the British intruders that they were hoping to come across.

*"Meine Freunde...ich bin hier drüben...Die Engländer haben mich hier gelassen."*

He spoke confidently and without the trembling and crackling that I had got used to in the last twenty minutes or so. He seemed like he was happy with what it was he calling out.

I began to wish that McKay was with us, as he would have known exactly what it was Maas was calling out. He would have known the exact moment to have pulled the trigger, even before Maas said something that he shouldn't have done.

For all we knew, Maas was telling them that we were here, how we were armed and exactly where we were hidden. He might have even been telling them to head back to their lines and call for more artillery, we were simply in the dark.

I thought of McKay some more, trying to work out what it was he might have been doing around about now. I looked at my watch. It was three twenty-six in the morning. Sleeping in all likelihood.

But then I wondered how easy it would be for a man to get some rest like that, when he knew that his court martial was looming over his head, now just a matter of hours away from starting. I hoped that he had had a change of heart, and that he wasn't happy in just resigning himself to a firing squad.

McKay had been born and brought up a fighter. He deserved to go down fighting if he could help it. There was not a thought that I detested more in the world at that moment in time than picturing McKay being led out at dawn, his arms bound and tied, before staring down a firing squad.

No man deserved to die like that. There was no such thing as cowardice when you had fought as bravely as McKay had done in the past.

The German began to call out, as confidently as ever, the false strain that he put into his voice just about convincing me that he was still feigning a far greater injury than the one that he possessed.

*"Kommst du? Bitte helfen!"*

But then, everything changed in a flash. Everyone heard it and, at the noise, everyone's muscles tightened dramatically.

*"Ja...Bleib ruhig...Dummkopf."*

I was sure that Lawrence had been the first to have heard it, the one that had been closest to the source of the voice. He peered over the top of the ruins, just enough so that only his eyes and forehead would be visible if a light was suddenly shone on him, even his rifle down by his side now to conceal himself for a precious few seconds longer.

Then, there was silence. An eternal one that felt like it was daring us to break it. But I was determined to keep a hold on it just for a few more seconds.

I wanted to try and enjoy my last few moments of life. But then, I heard one of the boots slip on a piece of rubble.

They were here. We were about to find out if Maas had kept his side of the bargain.

## 14

There was no real way of knowing whether or not Maas had been true to his word, but before too long, the sounds of boots on broken walls became even louder than they had before. They were inside the confines of the old farmhouse.

I held my breath and looked to the stars, as if they could give me some guidance or good fortune and everything else in between. They glistened defiantly behind the man-made curtain of dust that was slowly thinning out and turning to nothing more than wispy clouds.

It was odd to look at the stars, hundreds of thousands of miles away, and realise how small I would be in comparison to just one of them. And yet, they appeared so small, so insignificant, to my human eye.

It made me think of McKay and his trial, as I realised that to me, and most other people, the hearing was nothing more than a formality. But to McKay, this was the biggest thing in his life, it would decide his fate. I would be sad if McKay was sentenced to death, but I would still be alive. I would live, I would be happy again, I would still feel things. McKay would stop being. He would no longer breathe, no longer speak, no longer exist.

But then again, I supposed the same could be said of me in the next few minutes. Who knew what was about to happen?

My breath was still sucked in and threatening to make my whole head explode, but the tension suddenly dissipated when I saw a figure skulk past me, quite unaware and careless, his only eyes for the German soldier who had now feigned a moment of unconsciousness.

I waited and waited, as the German made his way over to Maas and began to check for his vital signs of life. His breathing, his pulse, the warmness of his skin.

Another figure passed inches in front of my face, so transfixed on Maas that he did not even notice the stench of my skin. He must have just put it down to all the corpses that were littered around the place.

Then another and another, until there were no less than four bodies standing around Maas, each of them trying something different to revive him. I hoped that he continued to play dead until we had decided that the moment was right, otherwise we could be found out before we were ready.

In the accentuated darkness, I could see the whites of the Captain's eyes, glowing in the darkness. I was suddenly filled with an intense warmness, as I saw that the embers behind his eyes had changed and were now roaring with the intensity of a newly lit fire.

We stared at each other for a few moments more, as I waited for his eyes to tell me something, to urge me to action. But nothing came. Not yet anyway.

I could hold my breath for no longer, as it felt like my whole body was about to explode under an almighty pressure wave.

I slowly let the breath escape from my mouth, consciously limiting myself, in case I released it all in one almighty gasp.

*Crack.*

*Cra-Crack.*

Three blasts, all of them from rifles, all of them from the British Lee-Enfield.

That acted as the only starter pistol that we required, as we each began to pick a target and make our way towards them.

I leapt from my hiding place, my baton, complete with spiky nails, hanging low behind my hip somewhere. As the first German began to turn around, I swung the truncheon up and into his face, with the same force and vigour like a batsman trying to make the boundary.

I left the truncheon hanging in the side of his face, as he let out the first bellow of the scrap, alerting everyone on the Western Front to something happening out in the farmhouse.

I made my way over to the second man, who had

foolishly dropped his weapon, throwing myself onto him and pushing him over Maas. Franck woke up with a start, as the wind was forcibly pushed from his lungs at the weight of two fully grown men suddenly landing on him.

I pulled the German off him for a moment, as I felt the Captain begin to dispatch of his second victim behind me.

Rolling the German round, I whipped the side of his face with the revolver, sending blood and teeth flying in every direction.

It was as his jaw cracked under the third and fourth blow that I decided to change tack. The Captain had ordered us to keep it nice and quiet, but Lawrence and Chester had blasted that one out of the water with three rounds from their rifles.

There was no point in prolonging the inevitable for this poor chap.

Turning my head over to the left-hand side, I pushed the revolver into his forehead and squeezed.

*Boom.*

The round seemed to echo around the quaking walls for a moment or two, as I slowly turned my head back to face the mess that I had created. Surprisingly, there was very little blood on me or him, but I knew that the carnage would be evident if I was to look at the back of his skull. Which I didn't have time to do, as there was suddenly another body on me.

The weight of whoever it was pushed me down into my victim, as if he was forcing me to look at what it was I had done. The boy's eyes were wide open and forlorn, his mouth hanging open in an eternal howl. I could still feel the warmth of his mouth and the slight odour of his breath, even in death.

The figure suddenly brought something heavy and blunt down on the back of my neck and I felt the blood rush to the site immediately, the bruising apparent straight away. My wind pipe felt like it had ruptured, and I found it incredibly difficult to breathe for minutes afterwards.

But I knew I had to fight on, if I was to give up now then I would be going the same way as all the other Germans that I had killed that night, and I didn't really want to be in the waiting line with them at the gates of hell.

I tussled and fought with the grip of the German, until I angled myself in such a way that I could get a half-swing on his neck. I connected just under his jaw, my knuckle smashing into his jawline before trying to punch through the skin of his neck.

I repeated the motions three or four times, trying to get the man off me, whose breath stank even more aggressively than his dead comrade.

Nothing seemed to move him however, each punch that I dealt brushed off as if I was merely a bee sting.

The German began to snarl, a deep, meaningful snarl, that told me everything that I needed to know. He was going to kill me.

Suddenly, revolver rounds began to snap and crack away inside the farmhouse, from which side and towards whom I had no idea, my only knowledge was that they *were* pinging around inside.

Being hit by one of them was the least of my troubles right now.

My revolver was trapped under my left side of my body, while my right side was completely weapon-less. I was in trouble, I had nothing to fight with.

I was in even more trouble when I saw that the nearest of my weapons that were to hand, was firmly in the grip of the German who sat on top of me.

I could see small droplets of blood begin to dribble off the end of the sharpened nails, as I rebuked myself for the idiocy of leaving it lying in one of the dead Germans.

He must have pulled it out himself, which meant that he would have known how far embedded the nails were into his comrade. He would have known how hard I had hit him. He would have known that I had meant what I had done.

He looked at the club for a second, as I tried one more, futile thrust towards his neck, which he avoided simply by leaning backwards.

*What a horrible way to die.*

I had fancied myself going out in an artillery barrage or in a hail of bullets, but not at the mercy of my own weapon. Especially one as barbaric and tortuous as the trench club. At least, I told myself, that the victims of that weapon had never known what was coming, I had never held it high above its victim's head like this German was doing.

He was tormenting me with it.

There was nothing more that I could do, so I did the only thing that I never thought I would do in my life.

I heaved myself up as best as I could, in an attempt to meet the club and take the fight to him. Then, as I reached the highest point that he would allow me to go, I spat. Straight into his eyes.

He flinched, realising what I had done, before letting out the most ferocious roar, and bringing the club high above his head.

*This was it. I was about to meet the same fate as so many others,*

*I probably deserved it. After all, I had just spat in another man's face.*

As the club began to descend, I thought of McKay, my sister, my parents, George Needs, the hip flask. Anything and everything it seemed, that meant that the falling club would take longer to get to my head.

Just as it came within an inch of connecting with my skin, a dark mass suddenly pulled the German from my body, one of the nails angrily ripping into the skin just under my eye and tearing it painfully. For a moment, I thought I would be blinded, but soon realised that my eyesight was perfectly intact.

The club hadn't come down on my head. It had only left a deep gash in my cheek.

I scrabbled to my feet, as a struggle took place between a tangled shadow, as one seemed to chase the other around the room.

That was when the gunshots began to sound. Muffled to begin with, before getting far louder.

*Bumf. Bumf. Bumf. Bang. Bang.*

The body on top of the struggle jolted each and every time the revolver erupted, being shocked into jumping an inch or two into the air each time.

After the final gunshot, everything fell silent. Everything was perfectly still once more.

"Check the bodies, make sure they're all dead."

Figures began to appear all around me, tugging at the other shadows on the ground and pulling them around to make sure they were no longer breathing. I could not see how any of them were, they were all either filled with more holes than a rabbit warren, or more knife wounds than a bayonet practice doll.

I could do nothing but lie there, struggling to get my breath back.

Eventually, my chest in all kinds of pain and my lungs threatening to shut down, I wheezed my way over to where the two bodies had tussled together.

Huge craters had appeared in the dead man's back, as the close proximity of the rounds had entered his body, obliterating anything in their path. They had done their job.

I rolled the body away to look at my saviour, who was wheezing and spluttering more than I was. His face was a fluorescent red colour, despite the greasy black that was slowly washing itself from the surface of his face.

"Hamilton..." I breathed, before being caught by a

shortness of breath once again. "Thank you," I coughed and spluttered, before turning away from him to get whatever it was at the back of my throat out onto the ground.

"Don't mention it, Sergeant. You would have done the same."

I looked around me. There were bodies all around us, some of them moving, some of them not, but at least three of them were already smoking.

I had survived, somehow. Again.

## 15

I slumped backwards, against one of the rickety old walls, as I finally allowed myself a few minutes of breathing, so that the nausea and vertigo could eventually pass over me. My shoulders heaved up and down, as if they were some sort of engine, pushing the air more than anything into my lungs, to stop myself from keeling over in a ball to die.

I stared up at the stars once again and just drank them in. I didn't think of anything for a moment, except that, even in their smallness, they were exceptionally beautiful.

I thought of McKay once again, and how I had wanted him next to me for as much of my fighting days as possible. I wondered if he was still awake and whether or not he had managed to give us any thought as we had journeyed out on another adventure without him. I was certain that he had done, which made me notice his absence all the more.

But, at the same time, I was eternally grateful that he wasn't with us and that he had avoided this particular little scrap. I felt like the tension that had festered between some of us in the last day or so, especially between Lawrence and Earnshaw, had been as a result of McKay's situation.

Lawrence felt like he was getting the punishment that he deserved, while Earnshaw was prepared to fight for him to the death. It was good that McKay was not forced to see that kind of tension.

I felt frustrated with Lawrence for a moment, the animosity and anger that he harboured in his heart over McKay's predicament completely unjustified, as he and Chester were quite clearly holding something back from being brought to light. He had been jumpy, panicky, so had Chester, which could have led to the whole thing ending up in quite a different outcome.

I had to bring it up. I heaved myself towards Chester and Lawrence and growled in their ears.

"What is wrong with you two? The Captain said to keep it quiet, he could not have been clearer."

"Sorry. We were a tad jumpy."

"You're telling me. I don't know what has happened with you two in the past, but either you leave it here, or you explain to me exactly what it is that is your problem. You will *not* risk our lives again like that, understood?"

My face was burning hot, a result of the fight but also the pure hatred that surged through my veins as I looked at the two Canadians. They were not bad men, in fact they were excellent soldiers, but they were damaged men. We all were. But there was a fine line between being damaged and being a liability.

Right now, they were both. They needed to pull themselves together.

There was an uneasy silence that suddenly started to stretch across the ruined farmhouse, as each of us slowly got back to normal and realised that the small scrap that we had been in might not have been the end of it, there could still be more on their way out to meet us. Especially as we had just fired off a series of gunshots.

I grabbed a rifle and leapt over to where the Canadians were sat, themselves already trying to strain their eyes as best as they could.

"See anything?"

"Nothing yet," Lawrence was sheepish, humble even.

"Do you reckon we'll see them again tonight?" Chester asked nervously.

"I hope not. I know one thing for certain, there's no way we'll be nabbing ourselves one of those canisters. That dream has turned to dust."

"The Captain's changed his mind?"

"Don't know. But I for one won't be going with him. I'm not on a death wish."

They both chuckled, some of the tension between us diluted as I shuffled away from them.

"Keep your eyes peeled chaps."

I coughed a few more football sized blobs of

phlegm, as I tried to recover fully from the beating that my body had taken. As I coughed, blood began to drip to the floor, at which point I realised that the wound under my eye had torn far deeper than I had previously thought.

"That looks nasty," breathed Captain Arnold. "Are you okay?"

"Yes, Sir. I'm fine thanks. Are you alright?"

"Perfectly fine, Andrew. We'll give it a few minutes to die down, then think about heading back. Alright?"

"Yes, Sir."

I was surprised to see that Franck was still sat there, as if I was him, I would have made off in any direction that I could find the minute that my captors had been engaged. He could have been back in his frontline trench by sunrise if he had wanted to.

"Nice bit of acting with that leg of yours."

"I didn't need to do much. It stings like a fire."

"I know the feeling."

I did not like him all that much, but I respected him. He had seemed like the kind of bloke that would do anything for whoever promised him the most, which had turned out to be true. But I wasn't sure that I would have been able to live with myself, if I carried the knowledge that I had helped an enemy team wipe out some of my compatriots.

It seemed like he would do anything for this girl of his.

"I hope you find your girlfriend. And I hope she's worth it."

He seemed to get the message and instantly looked down at the ground, gradually letting the gravity of the situation sink into his conscience. As he processed what had just happened, the prayer-like plea began to be muttered under his breath again, this time without letting anyone hear its contents.

I wondered if it was some sort of confession, or if it was done out of guilt.

Although I had detested what he had done, I did not blame him, as I probably would have done the same thing had I known that I would survive a little longer in the hands of the enemy. My own officers seemed to want me dead far more than they did.

He had clearly had enough of this war, evident in the way in which that he knew exactly what to do the second the guns starting bucking. He had pressed himself up against the nearest wall that he could find, regardless of whether or not it would stop a bullet. There was nothing more to surviving than that. It merely came down to how lucky you were.

*It was never down to that hip flask.*

"Is everyone okay?" I rasped, as I looked around the band of merry men that had seemingly made it through unscathed.

"We're both okay, Sergeant. Ready to move when you are," whispered Chester, speaking for himself and Lawrence.

"I'm okay," muttered Earnshaw, "bit of a headache though."

"Better rush you to the hospital as soon as you're back then mate," chuckled Lawrence.

Everyone seemed to be absolutely fine, apart form the odd cut and bruise and the wheezing lungs. Considering the odds, we had done remarkably well.

I reached for a packet of my cigarettes, to join with the others who were already puffing away. The Germans already knew that we were here, so to see a small chimney of cigarette smoke was unlikely to have been too big a revelation for them.

Begrudgingly, I chucked the packet towards Maas, who had started to eye me up. I tossed him a packet of matches also. Within seconds, he was puffing away on the finest cigarette that the British empire had to offer.

"Thank you, my friend. Thank you."

I bit my tongue for a moment, as I wanted desperately to tell him that we were not friends, we were far from it, but decided against it at the last moment. It would benefit nobody here if I was to make a comment like that one. We all needed to be as calm as possible for the next phase of the operation.

All of a sudden, a wave of guilt washed over me, causing me to spit my cigarette out immediately. I had forgotten someone. I hadn't checked with the one person who I should have asked if they were okay, and he had been incredibly quiet ever since.

"Hamilton," I half-rasped, half-whispered, "Hamilton?"

I found his body exactly where I had left him in the moments after the fight, where I had assumed that he was merely getting his breath back. But he was doing more than that. He wasn't just trying to get his breath back, he was fighting to keep it there.

"Are you alright, Hamilton? What's going on?"

He breathed heavily and slowly, as if he could not afford to speak right now, so instead I decided I would take control of him.

Running my eyes over his body, I could not see any visible signs of a wound or injury to his body. But that wasn't to say there wasn't one there.

"Come on, Hamilton. Tell me what's wrong. Just one word will do."

He heaved his chest in and spoke through a painful wheeze, as if it might have been his last breath altogether.

"Left...arm..."

"Left arm, left arm. Got it."

"I...can't move it...I..."

"Keep quiet. Stay quiet, mate."

Slowly, I lifted his arm for him, so it extended outwards fully. It was there that I left it, as his blood began to drip freely over the rocks that had become his bed.

"He's hurt?" Earnshaw asked as he shuffled his way over to the commotion.

"Yeah."

"Where?"

"I'm not sure."

I ran my hand up the inside of his arm, his whole sleeve a darkened pigment, damper than the rest of his kit. I reached along the length of his arm, but could not find where it was he was hit.

As I turned to face Earnshaw, my hand accidentally brushed under his armpit, causing him to shriek violently, his whole body convulsing.

"It's okay, Hamilton. Okay...It's his armpit," I announced, tentatively beginning to undo the buttons of his tunic.

"Pull the dressing out of that, would you?" I asked Earnshaw, passing him the tunic. We were going to need to patch him up and then move, as soon as possible.

The hole that had been sliced into his armpit was perfect, a deadly straight line that had looked completely intentional. I could not see how deep it was, but the thick, dark coloured, sticky blood that leaked from the slit told me that it was deep enough to be serious.

"Hamilton, you're going to need to be as quiet as possible. Bite down on this," I said, passing him the cloth bandolier that had housed my spare rounds of ammunition. It was the only thing that I could find.

"Here you are," announced Earnshaw, passing the dressing to me.

"Okay, Hamilton. Here we go."

I pressed the dressing into his armpit, forcing it up into the crevice of his pit, to the point where I felt part of it begin to pack into the hole that had opened up. Hamilton let up a distressed groan, which quickly passed as he began to succumb to the unconscious state that his body was begging for.

Still, I pushed a little bit further.

"Is it serious?" queried the Captain, leaving just the two Canadians up on watch.

"Yes, Sir. It's bleeding heavily and I have nothing to secure the dressing to. He needs proper attention, now."

"We need to head back immediately then," he sounded almost disappointed, as if Hamilton had let him down.

Hamilton's face continued to twist itself into all manner of shapes and variations, as he tried his hardest to deal with the pain. The accentuated features of his face, that stuck out on account of his set back eyes and slim stature, began to force themselves out even more now, as a heavy layer of sweat began to form on the surface of his skin.

"Yes, Sir. We need to get him out of here now."

"Right then, that's decided. We head back at once."

I was almost jubilant that the Captain had not had the say in the matter that he had been yearning for.

It meant that I was grateful for the fact that Hamilton had got himself injured.

## 16

I couldn't quite work out if the Captain was happy, annoyed or simply completely devoid of any human emotions. While Earnshaw and I tried our best to patch Hamilton up and get him ready to move, Captain Arnold barely even looked over in his direction, instead sitting and sighing, sporadically looking at his watch as if he was late for a very significant engagement.

I wondered if he was beginning to have the same thoughts that I was.

*Only five hours to go now until the start of McKay's trial.*

I tried to sympathise with him the best that I could. The way that I saw it, the longer that we stayed out here, the easier it would be for us to end up dead, which would have a dual disappointment to it. The first was that we would have failed in our operation and no one would ever know of the intelligence that we had gained that night. And the second, perhaps more importantly to us all, was that we would not be able to give evidence at McKay's court martial, meaning almost certain death.

"Hamilton, Hamilton, listen to me, listen to me," I gave him a couple of slaps around the face, just to make sure that he was still awake and able to take in what I was about to say. For a brief moment, he opened his heavy eyes.

"We're going to move in a minute, when we do, I need you to keep this arm pressed down as firm as you can go. Do you understand me? Repeat it back to me if you do."

"Arm...pressed...down on dressing...Got it, Andrew..."

I was taken aback. It was the first time that he had ever called me by my Christian name. But now was not the time to berate him for that. That could wait. I hoped that I would be able to joke with him about it in a few days' time.

I was trying my absolute best for the young posh boy who lay at my feet, not just because he had saved my life, but because he was a decent chap who did not deserve to die. I had been dreaming not half an hour before about how I had wanted his father to call him back home, so that he could see the rest of the war out safely, but I was beginning to come to the realisation that not even his father would be able to save him now.

"You ready, Ellis?"

"Yes, Sir. As soon as you are."

I pulled Hamilton's tunic back on, not bothering to do the buttons up, and pulled his webbing back over his arms, just in case he needed it later on. The straps would cut into his armpit, but it was the best chance he had of keeping the dressing in place.

"Right then, gents. Here is what is going to happen. We will leave in segments; Earnshaw, you are to leave first, just get back to our lines as quickly as possible and tell them of the situation. Next, I will follow, to clear the way for you three. I am expecting you to help move Hamilton, seeing as it was your lot that did this to him."

He raised an eyebrow towards Maas.

"Yes, Captain. Of course."

He was just grateful to be coming back with us, he clearly did not mind under what orders it was.

"You two," he looked over towards the Canadians, "I want you to wait here, to cover our backs. Just in case. Leave a ten minute gap between Ellis leaving and your departure. Got it?"

"Yes, Sir."

They looked at one another with a knowing expression, which seemed to be almost happy that they would be left alone again. They were used to working as just the pair, making all the decisions and knowing that if they got it wrong, it would be them who paid the price. Working as a team really did not fit their style.

Equally though, they were tinged with annoyance and frustration, as they knew that it was always the last men back to the line who got pinged in the back by a hidden enemy. I just hoped that their luck did not run out tonight.

"Here Hamilton, take this mate," said Earnshaw, as he prepared to leave first, "Hopefully I won't be needing that. I'll be quicker without it anyway."

He pressed his rifle gently into Hamilton's chest, before taking one last look at us.

"Right then, chaps. I'll see you in a bit. Good luck."

"You too."

The Captain left a very lengthy pause before finding his voice.

"Okay then, back to our lines. All quite simple really," he risked a smile, but it didn't feel quite right to return it, especially as Hamilton had suddenly become transfixed upon my face.

"You ready, David?"

He tried his best to nod.

The Captain left us, before we pulled Hamilton around so that we could pull him by his webbing. He winced as the strap found its way into the pit of his arm, but he was slowly becoming desensitised to the pain, which wasn't necessarily a good sign. If he could tell us when it really hurt, we could work out whether we were making it worse for him or not.

Our progress was incredibly slow, and I could make out the shape of Captain Arnold up ahead, impatiently stopping and waiting for us to reach the next waypoint.

He was crawling as the crow flies, so that we had as little manoeuvring as possible to keep Hamilton in as much comfort as possible. On the way, he was moving bits of old barbed wire and rotting carts that had been there ever since we had first arrived in Albert.

As we sloshed through shallow puddles and around long-dead men, I couldn't help but imagine all the dirt and grime that was infiltrating Hamilton as we pulled him along. I could only hope that the dressing was doing its job, at both keeping his blood in, but keeping the dirt out.

We began to tire quite quickly, the weight of any full-grown man taking its toll far more than I could ever have imagined. But I was coupled with the German, who was skinnier and weaker than I was, especially with the wound that had been gushing from his leg ever since his little theatrics.

"Nearly there, Hamilton. I can see our wire now mate."

I looked down at him.

"Hamilton?"

I put my ear to his nose. He was breathing, just about. But it was weak and irregular. He needed to see a doctor and as soon as possible.

I looked around panicked, trying to spot the Captain so that I could usher him over for some additional help, but I had lost sight of him.

*Where is he?*

He couldn't have made it to our lines already, could he?

We weren't far off. In fact, if I was to get up and run,

I would probably have been there in fifteen seconds flat.

But it was going to take far longer than that, with one seriously injured man in tow and another not faring too well either.

My heart began to pound faster than the rate of a machinegun, each beat pumping harder and faster than the last, until the point where I thought it would simply give up all together.

I began to get really flustered but decided there was nothing for it apart from to persevere.

"Come on, let's go."

It took us another three or four minutes before I spotted the Captain again, lying behind a pile of rotten old wood that had come to embed itself upright in the mud.

I began to tug Hamilton with a renewed vigour, suddenly picturing the strength with which McKay would have been able to pull him, with his short but incredibly powerful frame, like a locomotive engine, surging towards the British lines. If McKay had been here, I was sure that we would all be back in the British lines already. No doubt about it.

"Wait...Stop..."

"What's the matter, are you okay?" I said, turning to Maas, who had ordered me to halt.

"Not me. Him. He's gone."

"What? No. I've only just checked."

"Check again."

I looked at Hamilton's face. One eye was wide open,

the other as if it had tried to close but not quite sealed itself. Both of his pupils had widened to the point where you could barely make out what colour they had been. His mouth hung open in a pathetic yawn, which was where I pressed my ear in the hope of hearing or feeling a faint breeze as he continued to live.

But Maas was right. There was nothing.

Hamilton had gone.

I checked his pulse, just to make sure. I didn't want him to wake up in a few hours, all alone and confused. But there was nothing. Just a distant warmness that was gradually going to lose itself over the next few hours. By sunrise, he would be as cold as all the other men that had been left out there.

"I am sorry."

There was nothing to be said, we just had to focus on ourselves now.

"Here, take this," I said, passing Hamilton's rifle to Maas, who looked at it in bemusement. "You do know how to use it, yes?"

"Yes, it's just...I don't know...Never mind."

"Good. Let's get a move on then, shall we?"

Maas stared at me, bewildered at my coldness over Hamilton and the way that I had entrusted him with a rifle. But the way that I saw it, if he was to turn the rifle on me in that instant, then I would not have really cared much at all. I was losing friends quicker than I could make them. Before too long, it wouldn't have surprised me if I was on my own in the world.

As for Hamilton, it felt as though I had taken a

pickaxe through my heart. I had loved him dearly and, although he was a year or two older than me, I looked at him as if he was my younger brother. I had tried to teach him as much as I possibly could about raiding and, in the end, he had lasted a lot longer than the one mission that I had predicted for him.

He was a fine soldier. A fine boy. That was how he would always be remembered. By me, anyway.

At that moment, a series of gunshots rang out, and I heard the wayward shots just thump into the mud not too far behind us. We didn't have time to look back and see what was going on. The Canadians would just have to sort themselves out, they knew what they were in for.

Then, a few more rifle cracks. Followed by silence. Then, a grenade blast.

I couldn't help it, I simply had to look backwards.

I could see no movement, other than the dust cloud that had emerged from the front of the farmhouse.

I waited for a second or two, yearning to see the two Canadians come stumbling from the back of the ruins.

*Come on.*

But there was nothing. There wasn't going to be either.

*Three dead in as many minutes.*

*Just sort yourself out. Come on, be selfish.*

It wasn't a difficult request.

It's incredibly difficult to be selfless when everyone that you love is either locked up in a prison cell or recently deceased. When that happens, the only person that you can look out for is yourself.

*Your sister isn't dead or in prison. Neither are your parents.*

I really must write to them, I told myself for the thousandth time.

I could see our lines clearly now, as the Captain slid his way into the frontline trench, his odd little head bobbing around at the surface as he awaited our arrival.

I was feeling weak, tender and lower than I had ever felt before.

*I will write to them as soon as I get back.*

*If you make it back.*

As the thoughts left my mind, they were overtaken by one that I had not had for a while now, one that I had managed to keep supressed for the last few weeks. But it was a thought that I was going to find incredibly difficult to ignore.

It had been a tumultuous night after all.

I really needed a drink. I really wanted some of that paraffin.

## 17

In the event, I hadn't had time for a drink at all.

As soon as we had made it back into the frontline trench, we were whisked off back to our billets and ordered to get changed as quickly as we possibly could.

We had only been allowed a very brief 'goodbye' with Franck, our hospitable German prisoner, who was taken away by the military police almost as quickly as we were taken off by our own forces.

The Captain and I had been given next to no time to have anything that resembled a wash and, even worse for the Captain, he had still not had the time for a shave. Now in the daylight, it seemed like his beard had grown at least half an inch in the few hours that we had been out in No Man's Land. That was the stress, I reasoned.

But now, I could feel the sweat beginning to drip from every possible crevice in my body, doing nothing but making me even more aware of the grease and dirt that was coating every inch of my skin. I wondered if Captain Arnold was feeling the same.

My palms continued to sweat like they never had done before, my heart racing as I continued to panic about what might happen in the next few minutes. I hadn't felt this scared in years, if at all in my life.

I looked at the palms of my hands, which glistened sweetly in the functional room that I found myself in. They were still muddied slightly, with a little smearing of Hamilton's blood still sitting on them comfortingly.

My uniform was pristine however, the cleanest one that I think I had ever pulled on, every crease and tuck exactly where it was meant to be. It was the same for Captain Arnold as well. It was probably only because someone else had laundered it that it was in such a good condition. I never managed to get mine that good.

"You are Sergeant Andrew Ellis?"

I pulled myself upright and back into the room. For a while I did not feel the need to reply, responding only with a stare that ended with a repetition of the same question, but just a little more irate.

"Yes, Sir. That's me."

"You served as a Private at Neuve Chapelle in January with the Second Battalion of The Rifle Brigade, before being promoted to Corporal. All correct so far?"

"Yes, Sir."

"You were then transferred to join Captain Arnold's men, where you were then promoted to Sergeant. Have I neglected anything in this regard?"

"No, Sir. Nothing at all."

"Good. Good." He spent a few moments before looking up at me once again, clearly disgusted at the state of the man that stood before him.

I looked him boldly in the eye, in an attempt to try and unnerve him, but there was no real hope of that. The major sat coolly in his chair, as if he had been there a thousand times already that morning, flanked on either side by two, much younger looking Captains, who had apparently found their way to a nice cushy job this far behind the line.

*Hamilton should be the one sat there. He could still be alive.*

The table that they sat at was highly polished and overly long, stretching almost from one side of the room to the next, along the length of the far wall with an imposing looking window directly behind the three presiding officers.

McKay was stood over to my right, at the side of the room, sitting behind a battered old table that looked like it was from the days of Napoleon. Next to him sat a young, overenthusiastic Lieutenant, who fiddled with his fingers out of a desperation to do something.

Behind him, reminding him constantly of where he was, was the most stern-faced Company Sergeant Major that I had ever seen. I tried my utmost to avoid eye contact with him, as I convinced myself that I would turn to a pillar of salt the moment we locked on to each other.

"So, Sergeant Ellis, are you fully aware of the charge that Lance Corporal McKay is on here today?"

"Yes, Sir. Perfectly, Sir."

"And you are also aware of the plea that he has consequently entered?"

"Yes, Sir. He has pleaded guilty, Sir."

I had tried my very hardest to get him to lean the other way, as pleading guilty would almost certainly lead him to being shot, especially on the charge of treason and desertion that he was on.

I looked over at him as I responded to each of the Major's questions, hoping that McKay would see something in me that would make him have a change of heart. But there was no recognition of the torment that I was going through on his part.

He simply looked at me and smiled.

He looked well rested and presentable, quite the opposite to me, who had had no sleep whatsoever and was now presented before a court martial, with senior officers scrutinising my every move. I hoped that they knew of the circumstances, or there was a chance that the Captain and I would both be placed on a similar charge, just for the way that we looked.

I thought for a moment about how lucky McKay had been, to be able to get a full night's rest. At which point I felt quite betrayed by him.

*Why hadn't he been up all night? He had known that we were out. Why wasn't he worried about us?*

I tried my best to return a half-smile but found it difficult to when I looked upon his sorry situation.

Above everything else, McKay had no clue that Hamilton was now cold, lying out in No Man's Land, waiting for the earth to slowly swallow his corpse, only to be dug up the next time a trench was dug there.

"Do you have anything to ask the Sergeant, Lieutenant Bourne?"

The young man got up, as McKay's defending officer, who had questioned the Captain in search of some mitigating circumstances earlier on. He had not lasted more than three minutes before running out of things to say. At least it was getting things over and done with nice and quickly for McKay.

"Sergeant Ellis," he said, his wayward eye looking up at his singular eyebrow while the other looked in my direction. "On the night in question, it was your first time out with Captain Arnold and his men. Am I correct in saying that?"

"Yes, Sir. That's correct. Captain Arnold had met with me and another man earlier in the day."

"Lance Corporal Bob Sargent?"

"Yes, Sir."

At the mention of his name, I twitched, expecting at any moment for all the presiding officers to begin to raise their eyebrows in recognition of the name.

*He had been the one to tell them.*

But there were no such flashes of familiarity, just steely, unmoving glares.

"Could you tell us a little bit about that night, Sergeant? How did you find it, as your first time out?"

I replayed the whole night in my mind, experiencing every bullet, feeling every artillery shell, as if it was all unfolding in the courtroom. I could see myself again, fresh faced and energetic, disheartened by what had happened to my previous platoon, but raring to get back at the Germans all the same.

"It was awful, Sir. I had seen death before. But not like that."

I continued to tell them my story, not leaving out a single detail for the men that were around me. I did not want them to feel like they had been left out of this war. I wanted them to know every last detail.

"There were bits of men everywhere. Blood on a scale unimaginable unless you have been there."

By the time that I had finished, Lieutenant Bourne was as white as a sheet. I thought for a moment that I had scarred the poor man for life.

"So...would you say that first raid has affected you, Sergeant?"

*Do you mean did it push me to the drink, which led to the death of one of my best mates and almost led to my own death?*

"Yes, Sir. It has."

"And what is it like to do it night after night. With no real end?"

"Most of us go over hoping that tonight is our night, Sir."

"Can you elaborate at all?"

"With all due respect, Sir, I'd rather not."

"That concludes all of my questions, Sir."

The major nodded, before piling his papers together with a flourish. He stood up. We all did.

"We will adjourn for a short time."

We nodded and saluted as he, and his two pets followed him out of the room.

No one said a word for what felt like forever.

"How long do we normally have to wait?" asked Captain Arnold.

"Not really sure," replied Lieutenant Bourne, "I've never done this before."

"Tell me you're joking?"

"I wish I was...It's all rather exciting though, isn't it?"

"You should try No Man's Land, Sir."

## 18

"Thank you, gentlemen, take your seats."

I was sure that the major's voice had deepened by an octave or two while we had waited in the courtroom for him to return. It must have been in preparation for the sentence that he was about to carry out.

I looked across at the Captain, who nervously rubbed away at his ever-lengthening facial hair and tried to glean just a single element of confidence from him. But there was none there to take. He was as petrified of what was about to happen as I was.

The only person that didn't seem nervous in the slightest was McKay himself, who sat there quite chipperly, until he saw the two pitiful, exhausted faces that stared back at him.

That was the moment that I can pinpoint the realisation on McKay's petite, childlike face. He was about to face the death penalty.

Although I knew full well what was about to come

out of the major's mouth, I could not help but feel that there was still an ounce of doubt, that there was just the slightest possibility that maybe he would not issue the penalty to McKay. Maybe he might let him off with a lighter sentence, or completely. After all, he had been one of the most fantastic trench raiders that I had come across, and he still had every trait that was needed.

Plus, we were now a man down since we had lost Hamilton. Perhaps even more if the two Canadians had not made it back. Who knew how they had fared?

"Will the accused please stand?"

McKay, who struggled to his feet, had to hold one wrist tightly so as to stop either one from trembling terrifically.

"Lance Corporal McKay. We, as the presiding officers of this court martial have reached a conclusion upon which we have all agreed."

I knew what was coming, but my heart began to ache under the pressure that was building in my chest. I wasn't sure how much longer my heart could hold out.

I could see it sitting on the table, it stared at me and taunted me. But it was not until it twitched as it was played around in the major's hands, that I realised that there was no going back. The black cap was on its way to the officer's head.

I hung my own head in shame and disappointment. I could not quite face the reality of it all.

"Therefore, Lance Corporal Christopher McKay, it

is the sentence here of this court martial that you will be taken from here to the place from whence you came and there be kept in close confinement until tomorrow morning at dawn, whereupon you will be taken to the place of execution and there face death by shooting, until you are dead. May God have mercy upon your soul. Amen."

"Amen," came the reply from the two awful looking officers that sat either side of the major.

I could not bring myself to lift my head.

## 19

I did not want to look up. I knew that the Captain was doing exactly the same thing.

Tears rushed to my eyes as I was silently overcome with grief.

To lose McKay in this manner seemed like the biggest injustice in the whole world. He had been the most aggressive fighter, the most brilliant ally to have had and because of a few moments of madness, I would be forced to watch him as he was tied to a chair, a small piece of cloth pinned to his chest, as a priest read him the last rites.

McKay was not a coward. He was one of the bravest men that I had ever had the pleasure to have known.

I felt more for his parents, who would now become the outcasts of the entire village and likely lose their jobs. Their son, who had been the village hero, was now the damned. They would become the lepers of the village. No one would touch them.

I had lost Hamilton just a few hours' ago, it was likely too that I had lost both Lawrence and Chester also, but now I was faced with the possibility of losing so much more than that. McKay had been my dependant, the one person that had accepted me for the man that I was; an ill-tempered and volatile man, who plied himself with drink at every available opportunity.

He had got himself injured as a result of my neglect, as I stopped to top myself up while he was in the fight of his life. He had known all about it, despite the fact that I had never told him, and yet, he had found it in his heart to forgive me.

It was that compassion that he had shown towards me, that leniency, that I now urged the major to show in some way. But I knew that it was final. His decision would not be overturned, no matter how loudly I screamed.

I wondered if there was anything that I could do, maybe I would be able to swap places with McKay, or tell the court that it was me who had done it and he was merely covering for me. I dreamed about jumping in front of him as the order was given to fire or helping him to break out of prison in the most dramatic of fashion, but I knew that it was nothing more than a fanciful dream.

It felt like an hour had passed before anyone said anything and even then, I found it difficult to register what was being said.

I looked at McKay. His eyes were drooping and heavy, a window to his soul as it slowly threatened to bring him to his knees. There were no tears in his eyes, just a glare of total dejection and eventual realisation. He had been hoping for a miracle, he had been adamant that something would have happened to help get him off. He had convinced himself that he was going to be back with the rest of the team by sundown.

"However, it would appear that some of you have some friends in particularly high places."

The black cap was still on his head, but he had produced a small letter from his pile of papers, that he now began to tap on the table, as if it had undermined absolutely everything that he believed in.

"It has been requested of me that if I could find it in my heart to commute the sentence, then certain men in said high places would be most grateful to me and my colleagues here."

*Hamilton.*

*It had to be him.*

All that pressure that I had applied to the young lad had actually paid off, he must have penned the letter shortly after I had mentioned it to him. Suddenly, I was awash with grief and pain, as I thought about his cold and lifeless body, continuing to chill out in No Man's Land.

He would never find out about what his father had done for him. He had helped to get the sentence commuted, rather than having him recalled to the life that he should have experienced, and berating him for stealing someone's identity in the process.

I felt awful for Hamilton, as I knew how much it

would have meant to him, had he been able to witness the act of forgiveness and love that his father had carried out.

The major glared burningly towards Captain Arnold, whereupon the thought crossed my mind that he too, had some friends who stood at particularly dizzying heights.

*Could he have sent a letter to someone?*

I was sure that if he had, he would have mentioned it to me. But, then again, it wouldn't have been the first time that he had kept a secret from me.

"Therefore, at the request of this letter, Lance Corporal McKay, your sentence to death by firing squad is hereby commuted to serve a ten-year imprisonment in a military institution, whereupon you will be released to serve in His Majesty's army once more. Do you understand?"

The clerk in the corner began to scribble furiously, as he made a note of the change in circumstance.

My heart suddenly tinged with joy at the thought of McKay being free one day. Just a mere minute ago, he stood as a man condemned, but now, he was a free man, he would just be in the waiting room for a while.

"Yes, Sir. Thank you, Sir!"

The major slid the black cap from the top of his head, folding it neatly onto the table, in preparation for the next case that he would undoubtedly hear later on in the day. The two captains either side of him stared at it, in disappointment. It was as close to the death and destruction of war that they would ever get, and now the major was taking it away from them.

"I have done as the letter has asked of me. Now, I would like to make a few final, personal comments. I understand the great work that you and your men undertake, Captain Arnold. And I am sure I speak on behalf of His Majesty, and the rest of our nation, when I thank you for the unimaginable risks that you endure on a regular basis."

He turned to McKay.

"What you have done Lance Corporal is unforgiveable, an act which would have been utterly inconceivable for the vast majority of men that are out here."

McKay took a breath in to defend himself, but the major carried on.

"Having said that, the vast majority of men out here are not fighting under the same conditions as you are. They do not have the same rules. I accept that you were under a great deal of torment and stress at the time of the night in question."

He began to chew over a bit of leftover food that had become trapped in the back of his teeth, except that's what it looked like to me anyway. He retrieved it, before letting it sit on his tongue for a second, before swallowing.

"Therefore, it is well within my power and jurisdiction to commute your sentence further."

The clerk suddenly looked up from his table in the corner, furious that he was going to have to start writing on a fresh piece of paper. I could imagine that he had already started to pack up his things, so convinced was he that everything was done and dusted.

"Lance Corporal McKay, I therefore commute your sentence of ten years imprisonment, to the full ninety days of Field Punishment Number One, which is to be carried out from tomorrow at dawn. However, after you have completed those ninety days, you will be stripped of your rank and will no longer be allowed to serve under Captain Arnold again. Is that all understood?"

Again, I did not know how to feel. I felt happy, in part, as it meant that the waiting time to become a free man was drastically shorter for McKay now, than it had looked a few moments before.

But Field Punishment Number One was no walk in the park. McKay would find himself tied to something, a fence post or lamppost maybe, his arms outstretched in the cruellest of fashions. He would be there for two or three hours a day, for ninety days straight.

It was brutal. It was not nicknamed 'The Crucifixion' for nothing.

But the other side of my heart was horribly depressed. In ninety days, McKay would be a free man, but we would likely never get to see one another again. In all likelihood, he would be sent to an infantry battalion somewhere, where he would eventually be killed by a lucky artillery shell, or a wayward machinegun bullet. After everything that he had done too.

I had to remind myself about what McKay's outlook had looked like just three minutes ago. I might never see him again, I might never serve with him again, but at least this way, he could die with a little more dignity and honour than by a firing squad.

He was alive, for now, and that was all that mattered to me.

## 20

As I sat back in my billet, alongside Earnshaw and Captain Arnold, I breathed a sigh of relief that everything would soon be getting back to normal. As normal as it could be for a man that was in the middle of a war such as this.

I was fairly confident that, for the next few days at the very least, we would be stood down, our small force depleted so much that we would barely have been able to damage the old farmhouse ruins, that we had hidden in.

Lawrence and Chester were alive, just, caught out by one German soldier who had survived the brutal ambush that we had laid on them.

One grenade had been all that it had taken to almost rip two of the finest sharpshooters that the British army had to offer out of this world. I was glad that they had made it out, despite our differences. In fact, I was sure that Earnshaw was as well. The teasing helped to keep him sane.

I was hoping that we would be reunited with them soon enough.

For the moment though, all we could do was lie around on our beds, smoke and chat. Which suited me down to the ground.

"Another one?" asked Earnshaw, the chipper tones slowly making their way into the back of his throat. He was happy, far happier than he had been in recent weeks. Plus, he had just bought himself another ring. It was just as hideous as all the others.

"Where do you find those things?" I asked, looking at the browning and oversized ring that he had pulled onto his index finger.

"Not telling," he muttered as he pushed a cigarette into my mouth, "I've reserved them all for my family. I'm not letting you have a single one."

"Not that I would want one of them, Harry. They're hideous."

I laughed, as I pulled in the first few lungs of smoke that I had missed over the two minutes or so that I had not had one.

I felt lucky to be alive. I felt lucky for McKay.

He would have started his punishment now, a fair old time for him to reflect on what he had done and what could have been. As for me, focusing on the past was enough torture that I could have murdered a man and seen a firing squad as the better way out.

It had made us all feel better, now that our little

secret was out in the open and now very much burnt to a cinder. I felt as if a burden had been cut from my back, one that would have weighed me down for many years, had I survived that long. It was a secret that we had all promised to keep and one, that some, like Sergeant Hughes, had taken to the grave with him.

I was still not quite sure about Bob Sargent though. I was still unsure about whether that particular secret was in his grave.

I realised at that moment, that it had made me feel immeasurably better once I had got the whole thing off my chest. It had felt good when I had got the paraffin out of my system and back to something that resembled good health.

As I itched at the stitches that would now leave a permanent scar under my eye, I realised that I should continue in the catharsis, by writing a letter.

I had the time now, I had the means, but as I searched myself, I could not for the life of me find an excuse.

I pulled up a wad of paper and licked the nib of the pencil that I would scrawl out my thoughts with.

I would write about the things that were weighing me down, but not the ones that really mattered, just the minor ones, I wanted my sister to know that I was doing alright.

*Dear Elizabeth...*

I suddenly wondered what it was that I could tell her that would not be censored as it found its way to her, but that would equally not bore her and my parents to tears at their reading of it. I scribbled out what I had written and began to reconsider the whole venture.

I decided to change tack.

*To my dearest Betty (and the old things) ...*

That was as far as I got, as I was interrupted. Not by my own doubts or thoughts this time, but by the Captain.

"Come on, chaps. Look lively, we've been summoned to another briefing."

The letter would have to wait, perhaps until when I got back from whatever outing the brass had waiting for our depleted band of merry men.

*If I got back.*

### The End

Andrew Ellis and the Trench Raiders return in 'Long Forgotten' - Head to Amazon to buy now!

## GET A FREE BOOK TODAY

If you enjoyed this book, why not pick up another one, completely free?

'Enemy Held Territory' follows Special Operations Executive Agent, Maurice Dumont as he inspects the defences at the bridges at Ranville and Benouville. Fast paced and exciting, this Second World War thriller is one you won't want to miss!

Simply go to:

www.ThomasWoodBooks.com/free-book
To sign up!

# YOU CAN HELP MAKE A DIFFERENCE

Reviews are one of my most powerful weapons in generating attention for my books.
Unfortunately, I do not have a blockbuster budget when it comes to advertising but
**Thanks to you I have something better than that.**

Honest reviews of my books helps to grab the attention of other readers so, even if you have one minute, I would be incredibly grateful if you could leave me a review on whichever Amazon store suits you.

Thank you so much.

# ABOUT THE AUTHOR

Thomas Wood is the author of the 'Gliders over Normandy' series, Trench Raiders as well as the upcoming series surrounding Lieutenant Alfie Lewis, a young Royal Tank Regiment officer in 1940s France.

He posts regular updates on his website
www.ThomasWoodBooks.com

and is also contactable by email at
ThomasWoodBooks@outlook.com

 twitter.com/thomaswoodbooks

 facebook.com/thomaswoodbooks

Printed in Great Britain
by Amazon

56657521R00113